"Have You Made Any New Year's Resolutions?"

"Just one," he said.

Emma lifted her hands to Nathan's face, sliding her fingers over his bold, masculine bone structure and sharp, well-defined jaw line. Even in the darkened room he had an arresting face.

He tugged his bow tie loose and left it dangling, drawing her attention to his impressive chest. Heat poured off his long torso, seeping into her skin and setting fire to her better judgment. Her fingers tingled as she traced the muscles beneath his white shirt. He radiated power and vitality. The sensation of all that caged energy weakened her knees.

"What is it?"

His mouth brushed against hers, lingering just long enough to blend their breath. She tried to catch his lips, to compel him to kiss her hard and deep, but he pulled away.

"I'm going to spend the rest of my life making love to you."

Dear Reader,

I'll bet every debut author gets attached to their first hero and heroine. After all, we spend years putting them through all sorts of hell before they get their happily ever after. They become as familiar to us as those friends who share their romantic dramas over happy-hour drinks. I'm just that attached to Nathan Case and Emma Montgomery.

Growing up, I used to watch musicals and old movies with my parents. The heroes of my childhood were Cary Grant, Frank Sinatra and Errol Flynn. So, is it any wonder I gave my first Desire hero a little of Cary's dashing charm, Sinatra's amazing voice and Flynn's scoundrel ways?

Deciding Emma should make original fine jewelry was easy. I'm an art show junky and love buying from the talented artists in my area. Her journey to success required hard work and believing in herself. Two things I hope my daughter learns from me.

I hope you enjoy meeting Emma and Nathan. And if you can, support your local artists.

Cheers from Minnesota!

Cat

CAT SCHIELD

MEDDLING WITH A MILLIONAIRE

Recycling programs
for this product may
not exist in your area.

ISBN-13: 978-0-373-73107-7

MEDDLING WITH A MILLIONAIRE

www.Harlequin.com

Printed in U.S.A.

CAT SCHIELD

has been reading and writing romance since high school. Although she graduated from college with a B.A. in business, her idea of a perfect career was writing books for Harlequin. And now, after winning the Romance Writers of America 2010 Golden Heart® for series contemporary romance, that dream has come true. Cat lives in Minnesota with her daughter, Emily, and their Burmese cat. When she's not writing sexy, romantic stories for Desire, she can be found sailing with friends on the St. Croix River or in more exotic locales like the Caribbean and Europe. She loves to hear from readers. Find her at www.catschield.com. Follow her on Twitter @catschield.

To my daughter, Emily. Thanks for believing in me.
I couldn't have done it without you.

One

Sighting his quarry at last, Nathan Case dodged a waiter carrying a tray of champagne and navigated around a chocolate fountain. Twenty feet ahead, Emma Montgomery slipped through the cream of Dallas society gathered to celebrate New Year's Eve. Ever since arriving at her father's home an hour ago, Nathan had been searching for Emma, contemplating exactly what he intended to do when he tracked her down.

His options ranged from kissing her to throttling her.

He had yet to decide which way to go.

As if sensing the intensity of his thoughts, she glanced over her shoulder. A strand of hair caught on her lush lips as she scanned the party guests. Delicate fingers brushed long sable bangs back from her forehead, exposing the frown that pulled her brows together. She looked like a wild creature caught out in the open, unsure of where to flee. Then, her chocolate eyes locked on him.

Quick as a rabbit, she ducked around a potted palm and disappeared.

His heartbeat surged as he picked up his pace. He'd had women play hard to get before. The game sweetened their ultimate surrender. But Emma had taken the maneuver to a whole new level. If he didn't know better, he would think she was avoiding him.

Ridiculous, given what he'd learned today.

He passed the library where a rollicking sing-along was taking place, with two dozen people crowded around the grand piano to belt out Sinatra tunes.

He caught sight of Emma just before she ducked into the room and followed, glad to leave behind the throng drinking Silas Montgomery's booze and gawking at the mansion the oil tycoon had built as a testament to his wealth and power.

The two-story library with its cherry paneling and wall of bookshelves was more intimate than the colossal great hall they'd left behind, but not quiet enough for Nathan. He intended to have Emma to himself by midnight. He had no intention of letting anyone but him kiss her incredible mouth.

She stopped dead as he cut off her escape route. The noise level was too high for conversation, but Emma had little trouble communicating her impatience as he herded her toward the piano and nudged her into a narrow space between a blonde in a red halter dress and a short balding man whose attention was riveted on the woman's cleavage.

Nathan surveyed the blonde without interest. Although he appreciated a half-naked woman as much as the next guy, he wasn't a fan of augmented breasts. He preferred curves that jiggled. Emma's in particular.

His lips hovered just above her ear as he softly sang the lyrics that accompanied the romantic tune. He put his hands on the gleaming black instrument, trapping Emma between his arms. She stepped closer to the piano to avoid contact with his body.

With her luscious frame calling to him, Nathan locked his elbows to prevent himself from pressing his lower half against her round rear end. He almost groaned at the memory of cupping those sexy curves in his palms. Desire roared in his ears, drowning out the music. He lowered his head and inhaled her perfume. The scent wrapped around his libido, causing momentary amnesia. Why was he angry with her?

Then he remembered.

In the pause between songs, he whispered in her ear, "Your father and I had an interesting chat this afternoon."

Emma lifted her shoulder as a barricade. "Cody mentioned that you had a proposition for Daddy."

Nathan had a proposition for her as well. A proposition of a very different nature than what he'd discussed with Silas Montgomery.

"Did your brother tell you what we discussed?" he quizzed.

"No."

"Aren't you curious?"

"Should I be?"

Leaning down, Nathan nuzzled Emma's temple. "Your name came up."

She jerked away from his lips and glared at him, but before she could voice the protests roiling in her eyes, the man tickling the ivories played the first bars of "Come Fly With Me" and conversation became impossible.

What was going on? Emma certainly wasn't acting like a blushing bride-to-be. But he was convinced she'd been behind the terms her father had presented earlier that afternoon. Silas Montgomery couldn't resist giving his little girl anything her heart desired, and Nathan knew Emma wanted him. She'd certainly demonstrated that after he'd stolen her away from the Christmas party they'd been at three weeks ago. So why had she bolted the instant she'd set eyes on him tonight?

Across the piano, a round, middle-aged woman frowned at him, an expression made all the more dramatic because it looked as if she'd used a black marker to drawn on her eyebrows. He met her gaze hard, silently warning her to mind her own business. She shifted her attention to the bald man, who was now captivated by Emma's cleavage.

Nathan sucked in a breath and counted to eight before he mastered the impulse to bare his teeth at the guy like some overzealous guard dog. Instead, he focused on the familiar music, relaxed into the romantic lyrics that had caused generations of women to swoon, and contemplated the knockout he must marry if he hoped to do business with her father.

Nathan and her brother, Cody, best friends since college, had often talked about business opportunities that sparked their interest, but they hadn't discovered any worth pursuing until recently. When he and Cody had first discussed the idea of a joint venture between Montgomery Oil and Case Consolidated Holdings, Nathan hadn't anticipated marriage to Emma as part of the negotiations, but he couldn't say he was completely surprised that Silas had made it a key factor in the deal. The project would be a long-term undertaking, requiring huge amounts of capital from both companies. Cementing the connection between Case Consolidated Holdings and Montgomery Oil through marriage ensured that both sides were totally committed to the venture.

Emma would know that. And use it to her advantage. He should be flattered that she wanted him so much that she'd cooked up the scheme and persuaded her father to go along with it. And why wouldn't Silas agree? Once Emma was married, she became someone else's responsibility.

"You have an amazing voice," the blonde to his left told him. She smoothed her left hand across the piano's glossy surface, showing off the huge diamond adorning her middle finger. The bare ring finger proclaimed her availability. "And you know all the words."

Across the narrow space separating their bodies, Emma's spine stiffened at the blonde's blatant flirting.

"My mother loved Sinatra and played his music all the time while I was growing up. She used to call me her very own Rat Pack member. Although, I think her meaning had less to do with my singing and more to do with my knack for troublemaking."

The blonde gave a throaty laugh.

"You're trouble all right," Emma muttered.

Nathan grinned. He liked her humor. She was a terrific package: sexy and funny.

Thinking he had smiled at her, the blonde rotated her upper body toward him. Her low neckline gaped farther as she extended her right hand. One shapely leg slipped between the long slit in her skirt and grazed his thigh. "My name is Bridget."

"Nathan." He clasped her hand while annoyance radiated from Emma like fallout from a nuclear disaster. "How do you know Silas?"

He didn't catch Bridget's answer because his arm no longer blocked Emma's exit, and she'd seized the opportunity to run. As she turned to go, her chest brushed against the bald man's shoulder and his eyes almost popped out of his head. Oblivious to the commotion she'd caused, Emma offered him a brief apology as she slipped past.

Nathan gave the blonde a what-can-you-do shrug. Her smile became a pout as he turned to follow Emma.

She didn't get more than three steps beyond the library before he caught her. Nathan slid his hand around her waist and altered her direction, guiding her to the one place on the first floor where they wouldn't be disturbed by party guests.

"The last time we met I got the feeling you were looking

for a little trouble," he murmured near her ear as he herded her down the hallway to her father's study.

She eyed him as warily as a colt sensing the approach of a mountain lion. Perhaps she'd guessed what was on his mind. No man pursued a woman the way he had without wanting her naked and horizontal.

"Maybe I was," she said. "But that was then."

"And this is now."

At the end of a long corridor, Nathan opened a door, and ushered Emma inside. Dark paneled walls absorbed the single light source: a lamp perched on one corner of a massive antique mahogany desk. In a home office of normal size, a piece of furniture like this might have overwhelmed the room, but this house had been built to impress. A leather couch, with flanking chairs, sat before the carved marble fireplace. Texas landscapes adorned the walls, painted by one of Nathan's favorite artists of the early twentieth century. Unlike the delicate French antiques decorating the rest of the mansion, this room's rugged lines and leather furnishings suited the Texas oil magnate who lived here.

Nathan shut the door, caught Emma's arm and spun her around. Before she offered a protest, he backed her against the door. On the other side of the panel, voices and music blended into hazy, indistinct murmurs. Alone at last.

He leaned his forearm above her shoulder, letting his intent settle over her like a silk sheet. "Aren't you curious why your name came up?" he questioned, returning to their earlier topic.

"Not in the least."

"It seems that your father is shopping around for a husband for you."

"Damn." Her head fell back against the door, and the fight whooshed out of her. "He's been trying to marry me off since college."

"Why?"

"Because I'm a handful of trouble he wants to dump into someone else's lap." Bruises developed in her eyes, put there by her father's harsh opinion. "He's got this idea stuck in his head that I need someone to take care of me."

Being the pampered daughter of a billionaire was part of her charm. Nathan was looking forward to spoiling her rotten.

"What's wrong with letting someone take care of you?" he asked.

"Because the assumption is that I can't take care of myself." Her chin came up. Fire returned to her eyes, but her voice gained a ragged edge. "And that's completely unfair."

In the interest of keeping the conversation civil, Nathan resisted arguing that point with her. Even though he didn't see her brother, Cody, much since he'd gotten married, they kept in regular contact, and Nathan had heard all about Emma's escapades. The near-engagement to a fortune hunter, a sentence of community service after she'd been caught holding a friend's purse containing drugs, and a totaled Mercedes from driving home after a party in the middle of an ice storm.

Granted, she appeared to have settled down in the last few years, but her impulsiveness with him three weeks ago made him question whether she had truly grown up, or whether she'd just gotten better at keeping her activities a secret from her family.

"Have you told your father how you feel?" he asked.

"Yes." She expelled her breath in a rush. "For all the good it did me. When Daddy sets his mind to something, it stays set. He wants me engaged by Valentine's Day. Whether I like it or not."

And whether Nathan liked it or not.

He needed this joint venture with Silas to seize control of the family business from his half brothers. Neither Sebastian nor Max had any faith in his vision for their company. That's why the partnership with Montgomery Oil was so important. Not only would the new venture's cutting-edge technology put Case Consolidated Holdings on the map as an innovator, the future profits would ensure that the balance of power in the company would shift to Nathan. His half brothers would hate it, and there would be nothing they could do about it.

But first he needed to make the deal happen.

On a sudden whim, Nathan quickly unfastened Emma's diamond and sapphire earrings from her ears.

"Give me back my earrings," she demanded as he dropped them into his pocket

The last time he'd stolen her away from a party, she'd fought the chemistry between them, driving him half mad in the moments before her complete surrender. Afterwards, she'd raced off, leaving nothing behind but the evocative scent of her perfume on his skin. Tonight he intended to keep something she'd want to reclaim.

"Not yet."

Artfully arranged wisps of sable curls framed a heart-shaped face with exotic high cheekbones and a slender nose. Tonight she'd tamed her sumptuous brown waves into a fancy, upswept hairdo that drew attention to her elegant neck. Although he liked the way the style bared her lovely golden skin and the hollow of her throat, he preferred her hair loose around her shoulders, tousled by his hands.

He removed the pins holding her hair in its fancy updo. A rich, satiny curtain tumbled about her bare shoulders, stripping away another layer of sophisticated veneer.

"Nathan, what are you doing?"

"I should think it was pretty obvious." He feathered the tips of his fingers along her gown's neckline, grazing her skin.

"Can't we just talk?" she gasped, putting a hand on his chest to hold him off.

The heat of her touch seared through his shirt, igniting a thousand fires. His powerful need for her unsettled him. She made him wild. No other woman turned him on as fast as she did, or made him lose control so completely.

He sifted his fingers through silken waves of sable, twirling one curl around his hand. "If you'd bothered to call me back, we could have talked numerous times in the last few weeks. Right now I have other things on my mind."

"Here? In my father's study? Are you crazy?"

Lust surged at the notion of taking her hard and fast against the door, but he had no intention of doing that again.

Three weeks ago, his first glimpse of her in a dozen years had knocked him off his game. He'd gone to the holiday party, looking to relax and reconnect with another college buddy of his and Cody's. A couple of hours at one of Grant Castle's parties offered him the opportunity for some casual flirting with beautiful women. In fact, he'd been surrounded by five lovely ladies, all vying for his attention when Emma had strolled through the front door, her long, shapely legs bared by a black minidress that shimmered.

Her gaze had shot to him as if he'd released the wolf whistle hovering in his mind. When their eyes locked, all casual thoughts went out of his head. He targeted her like a jungle cat sighting a leggy gazelle and had her out the door and in his car before an hour had passed.

He'd kept his hands to himself until they arrived back at his condo. But once inside, his lips captured hers. He'd been caught off guard by their first kiss. He'd expected more expertise, not the tentative, sensual attack of her fingers against his face, through his hair. Emma acted like a woman who hadn't been kissed in a long time, or at least not one who had been kissed properly.

He'd gone slightly mad then. Nothing else could explain why he'd been too impatient to carry her to his bedroom and take the time to savor every inch of her skin. He'd burned for her and she'd matched his intensity. It amazed him that they hadn't set the foyer on fire.

The next time they made love it would be on a mattress, with her naked and sprawled out to await his pleasure—and hers.

She was a woman worth appreciating.

"Shall I tell you what I'm going to do to you?"

Her breath caught on a quick inhalation. "No."

Yet despite her denials, she didn't push him away. So he capitalized on her ambivalence, using words as a prelude to action.

"First, I'm going to strip you out of your very sexy dress." He grazed his knuckles along her side where the zipper started below her armpit and ended at her hip.

She made a grab for his hand, but he brushed her fingers aside. Her attempt to stop him had been halfhearted at best. Already her resistance was dissolving beneath the heat of this thing between them.

"Then, starting with the spot on your shoulder that drives you crazy when I kiss it, I'm going to take my time with you." He hoped this was working on her because he was driving himself crazy. "You're not getting away until I put my hands and my mouth on every inch of you."

He shifted his grip lower, drawing her tight against the unruly tension in his loins. His breath slipped out in a half sigh, half groan as she rotated her hips against the pressure of his hands.

"Are you wearing the black thong and strapless bra again? Or something different?"

His palms itched, and his fingers tingled as he remembered the way her nipples had hardened as he learned the shape of her full breasts. Tonight's midnight-blue dress seemed equally infatuated with her figure because it clung to her lush form with adoration.

"Let's have a peek," he cajoled, only half-serious. Last time, half the fun of their brief encounter had to do with how flustered she'd gotten at his teasing.

"No." The word broke from her lips in a passionate moan somewhere between protest and plea.

Her hand slid against his chest, finding his heartbeat. He wondered what she'd make of its increased tempo.

He cradled her face while he turned up the volume on her shivers and smiled against her skin as she tipped her head into his palm, giving him better access to her neck.

"Come on, let's go somewhere we won't be disturbed." He drifted his lips along her cheek, devouring her with languid, sultry slowness.

"I'm not going anywhere with you." Her objection ended in a murmur of pleasure as he leaned his chest against her breasts, pressing into her slowly. She stretched like a cat, rubbing against him, a dark, husky rumble deep in her throat.

It amused him that she continued to deny him. They both knew he would get his way in the end.

His lips descended until they were a hairbreadth from hers. "Why not? We were incredible together." One hand swallowed the curve of her buttock, coaxing her against the aroused hardness below his belt. "Feel how hot I am for you. I know you're just as hot for me."

The hand on his chest became a fist. "You have any number of women hot for you."

Is that why she'd been dodging his phone calls?

He smiled indulgently. "But you're the only one I want."

Emma lost the ability to breathe. His words intensified the ache inside her, a potent craving that left her shaky. And tempted. Oh, so tempted.

Flirting with him at Grant's party three weeks ago had seemed like a harmless lark. After all, he'd had no trouble resisting her ten years ago. At twenty he'd been broad of shoulder and delicious to look at, with a cocky charm that dried her mouth and left her at a loss for words. She'd pulled out every trick in her sixteen-year-old arsenal in hopes that he'd look her way. To her shock, it seemed to work.

Until the devastating one-two punch to her ego.

Her cheeks blazed anew at the memory of the day she'd put on her shortest skirt, a brand new pair of stiletto heels and borrowed one of her mother's push-up bras. She'd cornered Nathan in the kitchen and practically begged him to help her become a more experienced woman.

Then, he did exactly as she asked. Only not in the way she wanted.

Expression hard, gray eyes shot through with flashes of lightning, he'd held her at arm's length, laughed and told her to go wash her face and stop playing at being grown-up. And once he finished trampling her self-esteem to dust, he'd sauntered out of the kitchen. The following day he'd left for Las Vegas and hadn't returned to Texas until a few months ago.

She'd been thrilled to see him, believing she'd mastered the skills needed to cope with his vast reserves of sex appeal. Oh, how little she'd learned.

"I'm the one you want right now," she countered.

"You have no idea," he murmured, coasting gentle kisses across her eyelids.

If she let him have his way, how long before he moved on? Could she stand to spend every second of their time together waiting for the other shoe to drop? No. Better to leave things exactly as they were. The memory of their one night together would have to be enough. For both of them.

"Let's go back to my hotel." His hands flowed from her hips to her waist, the firm pressure fitting her more fully against his unyielding torso. "If you can resist screaming my name for an hour, I'll never bother you again."

An hour?

Anticipation swelled, drowning anxiety, as she remembered all too well the roller-coaster ride of screaming thrills awaiting her at his hands. She rubbed her thighs together to combat a mounting frustration. The way she felt right now, she'd climax before he had her clothes off.

He'd win. He knew it. Worse, he knew she knew it. Hell, she was ready to scream his name right here and now just to make the building pressure go away.

"Nathan, I'm not going to sleep with you again."

"Again? You didn't stick around long enough to sleep with me the last time. I'm looking forward to waking up with you in my arms."

His hand was warm and compelling against the small of her back. She lifted her chin while he nuzzled her temple. When his lips brushed the corner of hers, soft as a butterfly's wing, golden light spilled into her veins. If he had any idea how much she'd wanted to end up like this tonight, alone with him and poised to surrender, she would be doomed.

Don't do this. A rational voice shrilled in her mind while her bones melted, and her skin flushed. *You'll never get a chance to marry for love if you let him seduce you again.*

"You're afraid to give into this thing between us," he murmured. "Don't be."

"I'm not."

Letting go had been fun. She'd fantasized about him for years. But not one sizzling daydream had prepared her for the thrilling hard press of his muscles or the urgency of his kisses. He'd cajoled and demanded and she'd happily surrendered.

It was the aftermath that had terrified her. The treacherous longing to surrender control and let him dictate where the relationship went and how long it lasted. Discovering how fast she became putty in his hands had made it easy to avoid his phone calls.

His lips trailed wildfire kisses down her throat to the hollow where her pulse fluttered madly. "I promise to take it slow."

"How thoughtful of you," she said, injecting irony into her

tone. He couldn't find out how much she wanted to give in. "But I think you're getting the wrong idea."

"The wrong idea about what?"

"About what I want."

"And what is that?"

A man who would love her forever.

"Three, two, one…" voices shouted in enthusiastic unison. Noisemakers and horns generated a cacophony, almost drowning out cries of "Happy New Year!"

Listening to the party on the other side of the door, Emma wondered what the coming year would offer.

"Happy New Year," she whispered.

This was his cue to kiss her, but he didn't. He had such sexy lips, well-shaped with a fullness that teased and a wicked quirk that enticed. Anticipation lashed at her. She couldn't stop trembling.

"Happy New Year," he echoed, a smile in his voice. "Have you made any New Year's resolutions?"

"Just one."

"And that would be?"

She shook her head to clear the sensual net he wove around her with so little effort. "I'm resolved to be less spontaneous."

He chuckled. "And how is that working for you so far?"

"Not very well." She kept her tone dry, determined to master her nerves. "How about you? Have you made any resolutions for the New Year?"

"Just one," he said.

She lifted her hands to his face, sliding her fingers over his bold, masculine bone structure and sharp, well-defined jawline. Even in the darkened room he had an arresting face.

He tugged his bow tie loose and left it dangling, drawing her attention to his impressive chest. Heat poured off his long torso, seeping into her skin and setting fire to her better judgment. Her fingers tingled as she traced the muscles beneath his white shirt. He radiated power and vitality. The sensation of all that caged energy weakened her knees.

"What is it?"

His mouth brushed against hers, lingering just long enough to blend their breath. She tried to catch his lips, to compel him to kiss her hard and deep, but he pulled away.

"I'm going to spend the rest of my life making love to you."

Her heart fluttered against her ribs like a startled canary.

"That's a pretty big commitment," she said, unsure what to make of his declaration.

"On the contrary." His breath tickled her ear, redirecting her focus. She turned her head toward the lips hovering beside her cheekbone, but he pushed back, taking away temptation. "I can't wait to make you Mrs. Nathan Case."

Two

At his words, her heart hit her toes. Mrs. Nathan Case?

"What?" She wheezed, unable to breathe. "Have you lost your mind?"

Her hands left his chest and settled on her temples, where a jackhammer had started drilling into her brain.

"Hardly."

"This isn't because of the other night, is it? Because I assure you, one night of sex does not require a noble gesture on your part." She leaned forward and stage-whispered, "I wasn't a virgin."

A low chuckle rumbled out of his chest. "You sure didn't behave like one."

She let his comment pass unanswered while scrambling to make sense of what he'd just proposed. Unfortunately, she found it almost impossible to think rationally while the scorned sixteen-year-old inside her whooped with triumph. She smothered young Emma's enthusiasm and concentrated on reality.

Marry Nathan? Impossible. His ability to make any woman feel special did not make him marriage material.

"My father put you up to this, didn't he?"

"It's what we talked about this afternoon." Nathan's eyes narrowed. "He thinks it's past time you married."

"To someone I choose."

White teeth flashing in a cocky grin. "Got anyone in mind?"

Understanding dawned. She gasped in horror. "You thought I chose you?" An unsteady laugh escaped her. Oh, the humiliation. "I don't want to marry you," she said, keeping her tone slow and deliberate so he wouldn't misinterpret her meaning. "I don't want to marry anyone. Not right now."

Not without love.

"Your father seems pretty determined."

"You have no idea," she muttered. "But it's not happening."

Looking past Nathan's imposing shoulders, Emma eyed her father's enormous study and wished they were using more of it for this discussion. Speaking sensibly about all the reasons why they shouldn't get married would be easier without Nathan's gorgeous, muscular body trapping her against the door.

In an instant, she plummeted back in time to three weeks ago, when she stood pinned against a different door, her heart thudding madly, her senses alive while he thrust into her. With absolute authority, he had stripped her defenses, made her crazy with wanting and done things to her body that left her in a panting, spent puddle, craving more.

Emma pushed away the memory, locked her knees when they threatened to buckle and marshaled her resentment.

"Why would you agree to something like this?" she demanded.

"Case Consolidated Holdings wants to do business with Montgomery Oil."

"Daddy made our marriage a condition of the deal."

A business deal. She might have guessed. A howl rose in her chest. She clenched her teeth together to contain it. How could her father do this to her again? Hadn't he learned anything from the last time he tried meddling in her love life?

The summer she graduated from college she'd been engaged to an up-and-coming executive at Montgomery Oil. Imagine her surprise when she discovered that the reason for Jackson Orr's rapid advancement had to do with the deal he had struck with her father when he'd first started dating Emma. Jackson would move up the food chain in exchange for marrying her. When she'd found out, she'd broken her engagement and determined never to repeat her mistake.

"It must be one hell of a business deal," she grumbled, reaching over to flip on the lights.

Floor lamps chased away shadow. She blinked as her eyes adjusted to the brightness.

"The biggest one I've ever done."

"Then I guess marrying me is a small price to pay." The bitter taste of the words gave her tone a sharp bite.

"What's wrong?"

Her spirits drooped still lower. With a big business deal on the line, Nathan wouldn't be receptive to her pleas to turn her father down.

"I don't want to marry you like this."

"Like this?" he echoed dryly, picking up on how those last two words had betrayed her. "Is there some other way you'd like to marry me?"

Emma ignored the gleam in his eye. "I don't want to marry *anyone* like this." She didn't want to marry a man her father could manipulate. She couldn't respect such a man, and she knew she'd never trust him. "I resent being used as a bargaining chip in my father's deal with you."

"And I don't like being a pawn in your father's attempt to

control you," Nathan countered without heat, speaking as if he found the whole mess completely reasonable. "However, I suggest we make the best of the situation we find ourselves in."

His eyes burned with sexy intent as he located her gown's side zipper and slid it down. Before she voiced a protest, he stroked the straps off her shoulders. Her breath rushed out as she caught the dress before it fell. Her dress. Her defenses. Let one drop and the other would follow.

"Let me remind you how amazing we are together," he coaxed, sliding his lips into the spot on her shoulder he'd mentioned earlier.

"I don't need reminding, Nathan." Anxiety and anticipation fluttered in her midsection like drunken fairies. Although she couldn't shake her misgivings about his reasons for marrying her, the memory of his body mastering hers proved a powerful aphrodisiac. Marriage to Nathan would be like bronco riding: dangerous, exhilarating, uncertain. He would trample her heart, oblivious to the damage he'd inflicted, then race off to take on his next challenge. "But great sex isn't enough to base a marriage on."

He reached out and took her chin in his fingers to turn her face toward him. "It is if we don't indulge in unrealistic expectations."

She almost laughed.

In her darkest moments, when she'd contemplated her life if forced to go along with her father's plans, she'd pictured herself living the way her mother had, married to a businessman who worked long hours. She'd imagined herself spending her mornings shopping, followed by lunch at the club. Eventually, she'd indulge in a torrid affair with her golf coach or her daughter's French tutor. From observing others in their social circle, she'd assumed that she and her husband would live completely separate lives, coming together for business dinners and parties. Sex would be infrequent and only if she became sufficiently tipsy.

That was not the life she would have with Nathan Case, a man who left her weak-kneed and wanting with a look. For him, she'd pore through lingerie catalogs and work out at the gym to make sure she maintained her perfect figure. She saw herself planning luscious dinners for two and vacations to exotic locales. He would become her life, her obsession.

Emma shivered.

And what would she get in return? Would he be a faithful husband? Or would he indulge in extramarital affairs that would drive her to become like her father: Suspicious and watchful to the point where she drove him away? She'd watched her mother grow more and more miserable until Emma's junior year of high school, when she'd filed for divorce and moved to Los Angeles. She'd never remarried, and Emma often wondered if her mother was less afraid of losing her alimony than she was of risking her heart again.

Recalling his flirtation with the blonde in the library, doubts marched in and rang a warning bell.

"Unrealistic expectations?" she echoed. "Such as fidelity?" There, she'd said it.

"I intend for this to be a real marriage, Emma." Lightning danced in his gray eyes. His fingers slipped whisper-soft against her cheek. "You will be the only woman in my bed."

But what about his heart? How could a marriage be real without love?

Emma fought the panic trembling through her as she considered what sort of emotional seesaw awaited her as Nathan's wife. When her father had barred access to her trust fund ten months ago, complaining that the amount she spent on clothes and shoes proved she had no grasp of fiscal responsibility, she thought he was just trying to teach her a lesson. She never truly believed he'd force her to marry someone.

Reaching to fidget with her jewelry, Emma tugged on her earlobe and recalled Nathan pocketing the sapphire and diamond drops. They were one of her earliest designs. She'd dabbled at making jewelry since graduating from college, but a two-year stint as a goldsmith's assistant had dampened her enthusiasm for executing other people's designs. But when her father cut her off, she'd stubbornly decided to live on what she could make selling her own line of jewelry.

She realized after six months of slow sales that even if she lived without luxuries like designer fashions and spa visits, making enough to pay her mortgage, put gas in her car and food in her refrigerator would require her to work a lot harder than she ever had. And not just for a year, but for the rest of her life.

Or she could get her trust fund back. If she did what her father wanted and got married. Within one year. It was the one condition he'd put on restoring her funds.

She was tired of fighting. Fighting her father's will. Fighting the temptation to spend money. Fighting to pay her bills. This year had been hell. It would be so easy to quit. To do what her father wanted. Marry Nathan. Let him take care of her. No more eyestrain or aching muscles from sitting at her worktable for hours at a time. No more fretting over whether she could afford to keep her membership at her favorite yoga studio.

Emma straightened her spine. "May I have my earrings back?"

"I think I'll hold on to them for a little while."

"Why?"

"You disappeared out of my life three weeks ago without looking back. I want to make sure that doesn't happen again."

"I didn't disappear." But she had. The flash fire of desire

between them had sent her scurrying for cover like a startled rabbit. "Please, Nathan, can't we talk about this tomorrow? I'm tired, and I need time to think. Let's meet for breakfast in the morning."

Her weary defeat must have reached him because his hands fell away. He backed off enough to let her open the door and watched in silence while she zipped up her dress.

"I'll pick you up here at ten." Powerful and confident, dangerous and sexy, the combination sabotaged her resolve to walk away without a backward glance.

"Ten. Sure." She fled before he could stop her. She didn't think she had enough strength to resist him one more time. She had to get out of here. Tonight.

Racing up the back stairs, her heart pounding in fear that he might change his mind and follow her, she reached the second floor and paused to catch her breath when she was confident he'd let her go.

The wide hallway in front of her wrapped around the four-story great hall, circling upward to a dome painted with clouds. Her father had spent $50 million to re-create a little slice of French drama on the two-hundred-acre estate north of Dallas. The forty-thousand-square-foot mansion took its inspiration from Versailles both in style and grandeur with pastel walls and ornate French antiques throughout. It had taken almost three years to build, thanks to her father's obsessive need to oversee the tiniest detail, but it had kept his mind off his divorce from his fourth wife and granted Emma a respite from his nosing into her life.

Unfortunately, nothing good lasts forever. And when the last piece of furniture had been delivered at the beginning of February, Silas had once again turned his attention to his only daughter.

"And he complains about my spending," she grumbled.

The party didn't sound as if it was winding down. She neared the rail and peered below. A moving, brightly colored mosaic of elegant gowns and glittering jewels made her dizzy. Emma backed away and placed her hand over her churning stomach.

"There you are."

Emma turned in the direction of her father's voice. He strode along the hallway in her direction, his long legs eating up the distance between them. At sixty-three, he had the athletic build and energy of a man twenty years younger. He used his height as well as his strong personality to intimidate business associates and family members alike.

"I saw you and Nathan together." Her father eyed her mussed hair. "Have you talked?"

"Oh, we talked all right," she muttered, her cheeks warming.

"Wonderful. Come downstairs. I want to announce your engagement."

Emma hated confrontation. Growing up, she had learned to keep her head down in the ongoing battle between her parents. Clasping her hands together, Emma gathered her resolve.

"Not tonight, Daddy. I'm tired."

"Nonsense. It will just be a quick announcement and a toast to the two of you."

As much as she hated taking on her father, she was determined to stand her ground on this issue. "There is no engagement."

Silas Montgomery's blue-green eyes blazed. "Didn't he ask you to marry him?"

"He told me we were getting married. I told him we weren't." Resentment burned, giving her courage. She had to find some way to escape her father's plans for her. Whatever it took, she had no intention of becoming Mrs. Nathan Case. "I'm not going to marry him as part of some business deal between you two."

"Last Valentine's Day, I gave you a year to find someone

to marry. That time is almost up, and you haven't settled on anyone. So I found someone for you."

"I don't want to marry Nathan." Her father and Nathan were evenly matched in stubbornness, arrogance and lack of concern about her feelings in this matter. "In fact, he's the last man in the world I would pick to marry."

Her father frowned at her aggrieved tone. "That's not the impression I got from the conversation between you and Jaime at Christmas."

Emma groaned. As if this entire night wasn't humiliating enough, now she'd learned that her father had overheard her telling her sister-in-law about leaving Grant's party with Nathan and what had happened afterwards?

"You were eavesdropping?"

"You weren't exactly keeping your voices down."

"I thought we were alone in the house."

"I came back to get some papers." Her father's handsome face reflected little compassion. He was dealing with her with the same ruthless determination he brought to all his business dealings. "I know you've liked Nathan for a long time. I remember how you behaved when he used to visit from college.

So did she. Emma's cheeks burned. "I was sixteen. I didn't know what I wanted."

"And now you're twenty-eight. It's time you figured that out." Her father tugged on his cuffs, signaling the end of the discussion. "Nathan will make a good husband for you."

"I don't love him. He doesn't love me."

"But he will marry you."

"Because you're blackmailing him the same way you're blackmailing me." The edges of Emma's vision began to darken. She focused on her father's bow tie to keep from being swallowed up by helplessness. "Don't do this. It's not fair to either of us."

"You need someone to take care of you. Nathan is the man to do it."

"I don't need someone to take care of me."

"Yes, you do. You've never worked, and because you've never earned your own money, you spend without thought. I hate to think what would happen if you weren't limited by an allowance. And from what Cody tells me, your loft in Houston is a disaster. I've looked out for you for twenty-eight years, it's time I turn the job over to your husband."

Her loft wasn't a disaster. It just needed a master bathroom, a new kitchen, all new wiring and plumbing. She'd bought it shortly before she'd lost access to her trust fund. Her jewelry business barely covered her necessities. She had nothing left for remodeling.

"I don't need a husband. I can take care of myself. My jewelry business is taking off." A major exaggeration, but necessary if she was going to convince her father to give up on marrying her off.

"How much do you have left of the $100,000 I gave you last February?"

"Most of it." Emma refused to be more specific. She'd been in denial the first few months after being cut off and hadn't yet learned to be frugal. Giving an accurate number would reinforce her father's opinion about her frivolous spending.

"More like two-thirds of it," her father countered.

A mad, ridiculous notion sparked. "What if I had all of it?"

Her challenge ignited a speculative look in her father's eye. He loved making deals. "What do you mean?"

Yes, what did she mean? She wanted to retract her words, but it was too late. Backing down now would only give her father more reason to think she was flighty. "You say I can't take care of myself and earn a living. I say you're wrong." Emma gathered a deep breath and plunged forward. "What if I replace the entire hundred thousand by Valentine's Day?"

"How are you going to do that in six weeks?" Her father laughed.

"By selling my jewelry."

He shook his head. "You'll never do it. You're good at spending money, not making it. You don't have the drive to work hard and succeed."

Her heart constricted. Paralyzed by his scornful words, she felt smothered by all the mistakes she'd made in her life. Was it too late for her to change how her father perceived her? And what if she didn't try? It was either a loveless marriage to Nathan or learning to live on what she earned. Both sounded dreadful.

"But if I do," she persisted, her voice strengthening as her determination grew, "will you give me back my trust fund?"

Her father snorted. "I've seen the balance in your account. You won't be able to put the money back."

He was probably right, but she had to try. "I can and I will." She hoped she was displaying a great deal more confidence than she currently possessed. The task she'd set for herself made her stomach twist with anxiety. "One more thing. When I replace the entire hundred thousand, you'll also agree to stop meddling in my life." She stuck out her hand. "Deal?"

"As long as you don't borrow the money from anyone to bring the account balance up, we have a deal." Her father swallowed her hand with his and squeezed gently. His smile softened. "I'm only doing what I know is best for you."

"It's what you think is best for me," she retorted, pulling free. "And you're wrong." Her insides felt like jelly. What had she just agreed to do? "Now, you'd better get back to your guests."

"Are you coming down?"

Emma shook her head. "I'm driving back to Houston tonight."

"It's too dangerous to be on the roads at such a late hour."

It was far more dangerous for her to stay. "I'll be careful."

He frowned. "Emma—"

"One way or another, in six weeks I'm no longer your responsibility, Daddy," she said. "It's past time you start letting go."

"Of course it is." He kissed on the top of her head and retreated down the hall.

In her bedroom, Emma stripped out of her dress, being extra careful with it even in her haste. She'd borrowed both the dress and her shoes from Jaime, and would never forgive herself if she returned the designer original with any damage. As she zipped the gown into its protective bag, she contemplated her shift in perspective. A year ago she wouldn't have taken such care with her clothes. Any tear, stain, sometimes even a single wearing would prompt her to shift the outfit to the back of her closet. Funny…what Jaime had given her with so little concern, Emma now treated like a magical gown from her fairy godmother.

Thank goodness this dress hadn't disappeared at the stroke of midnight. A wry smile formed despite her turbulent emotions.

She donned jeans and a sweater, and then tossed the rest of her clothes into her overnight bag. Until her encounter with Nathan, she'd intended to stay the night, but after what had almost happened between them again, she needed some time to think, and the four and a half hours back to Houston would be just about right.

She didn't worry about falling asleep at the wheel. The encounter with Nathan ensured that the adrenaline pumping through her veins would keep her awake. As for being sober, she'd wanted a clear head in case he'd shown up tonight and hadn't allowed herself a single sip of champagne.

Feeling like a cat burglar, she hugged the wall as she descended the back stairs. She pictured her earrings resting in Nathan's pocket. What a lousy thief she would make, coming away from the house with lighter pockets than when she'd arrived.

Not until she turned left out of the driveway and followed the moonlit road back to the highway did the pressure in her chest lessen. Whatever it took, she'd put the money back in her account. She'd prove to her father that she could take care of herself and avoid the marriage net he'd woven to snare her. Nathan Case would have to figure out some other way to do the deal with Silas Montgomery.

"What do you mean she's not here? When did she leave?" Nathan glared around the quiet, empty cavern of a foyer that showed no signs it had been occupied by party guests a few hours earlier.

The maid clasped her hands before her. "I'm not sure."

"Hey, Nathan." Cody Montgomery trotted down the grand staircase. Dressed in jeans and a navy sweater, he advanced with a huge smile. "What are you doing here?"

The maid faded away as Nathan shook his best friend's hand. "Your sister and I were supposed to have breakfast this morning."

"Are you sure? Dad told me she headed back to Houston last night."

"Quite sure," Nathan said, indulging in a frustrated exhale. She'd disappeared on him again. He should have listened to his instincts last night and persuaded her to go back to his hotel room with him. "We had some things to discuss."

"Like setting a wedding date?" Cody chuckled as Nathan raised his eyebrows. "Dad told me you two are getting married. Never thought I'd see the day when you'd finally admit my sister has had you wrapped around her finger since she was sixteen."

Nathan held a growl between his clenched teeth while his best friend had a good laugh at his expense. "I wouldn't go that far."

Cody frowned. "But you love her."

Nathan wasn't surprised by the question. After five years of marriage, Cody and Jaime were still crazy about each other as they awaited the birth of their first child. Nathan wasn't sure what sort of water the two were drinking, but he intended to stick with whiskey.

"You know how I feel about love," Nathan said. He wasn't looking to fall into that trap. "It's never going to happen for me."

"But you're getting married." Cody gaze shifted away from Nathan. With a glance over his shoulder, he edged Nathan toward the front door, but didn't speak until the two men stood outside in the brisk January wind. "Does Emma know you're not in love with her?"

Nathan wasn't going to lie to his best friend. "She knows."

"I can't believe it's okay with her. After watching her mother's marriage to Dad fall apart, she's pretty determined not to marry unless the guy's crazy in love with her."

Cody made no secret of his belief that Silas's third wife had married her billionaire husband for financial rather than romantic reasons.

"She'll come around."

Cody shot his friend a skeptical look. "I don't think she will. You've been on her radar since she was a teenager, but she's got this whole fairy-tale happily-ever-after thing going. She's not going to marry you unless she thinks you're madly in love with her."

"Have a little faith in my powers of persuasion." Nathan offered his friend a slow grin.

A grin that faded as he strode to his car and gave his best friend a farewell salute. Cody's words poked at him like a burr long after the wheels of the BMW 650i coupe hit the main road.

Love.

Emma wasn't going to marry without it. Nathan wouldn't marry with it. Stalemate.

He wasn't sure when he'd decided that he'd never let himself go down that path. Had it been the Christmas morning when his mother burst into tears because he'd asked why his father didn't spend any holidays with them? He'd been eight that year. Or maybe when he turned ten and Brandon Case's wife had shown up to see for herself what sort of "whore" her husband had taken up with. His mother had cried for three hours straight after that. The next day she'd slapped him when he said he hated his father and hoped he rotted in hell.

Love made people miserable. It led to expectations. Expectations led to disappointment. Disappointment led to infidelity. Infidelity led to divorce. Except for Cody, all his friends had cheated on their wives or been cheated on. And they'd all started out madly in love.

He was an hour south of Dallas when his cell rang. He engaged the car's hands free system. "Hello."

"Hey, Nat, how'd it go?"

Hearing Max's voice, Nathan restrained a snarl. He could tell from his older brother's overly cheerful tone that he'd called expecting to hear that Nathan had failed. "It went fine."

"So, Montgomery is doing the deal?" Max's voice lost some of the good humor.

If his half brothers found out about the strings Silas had attached to the deal, Nathan would never hear the end of it. He intended to get the contracts signed without that happening.

"There are a few bugs to work out, but I'd say things look pretty good." Nathan relaxed his death grip on the steering wheel.

In his early twenties, he'd spent almost a year on the

poker tournament circuit, learning how to read people and to hide his thoughts. In the championship game, he bluffed two of the best poker players in the country and won half a million dollars. The skills he'd picked up during that time had come in handy these last six months working with his half brothers. He'd learned a long time ago never to let them see him sweat.

"But you don't have a signed contract," Max persisted, regaining his cockiness.

Nathan ground his teeth. Leave it to the middle Case brother to point that out. "As I said, there are a couple details still under negotiation."

"You were pretty sure you'd come back with a signed contract. Wasn't Montgomery impressed with your proposal?"

Nathan bristled at the implied insult. His brothers had developed their business acumen in the boardrooms of Corporate America. Nathan had taken an entrepreneurial approach. He'd grown his millions in the stock market and from venture capital investing. No matter how legitimate his investments, Max and Sebastian refused to give him credit for having a strong business sense. They couldn't get past the fact that his fortune had grown from the seeds of his poker winnings.

"Silas is looking over the numbers. He'll have an answer for me in six weeks." Valentine's Day. He hadn't understood the significance of Silas's choice of date until Emma explained her own deadline to him.

"That long? He's probably no more comfortable with the risk than Sebastian and I are. Two hundred million is a big chunk of our assets. If you're wrong, we stand to lose everything."

After their father's retirement, Sebastian and Max had changed Case Consolidated Holdings' business strategy from high-risk to ultraconservative. Nathan would be the first to admit that their father's obsession with huge profits had led him to make some dicey deals, but his brothers had overreacted.

And because they had, Nathan's ideas for moving forward by joining with Montgomery Oil to create a new company instead of continuing to buy existing companies had been met with skepticism.

"I'm not wrong," Nathan said.

He'd been a fool to let his father talk him into coming to work with his brothers. Brandon Case had been out of his mind to think Sebastian and Max needed him. They only needed each other. And their safe little strategies.

"You feed on taking risks," Max said. "It's like you get high from it."

"Any risks I've taken in business have come after a lot of careful analysis."

Max snorted. "Is that what you did at the poker table? Careful analysis?"

Nathan hated having his hard work reduced to little more than fortuitous circumstances, but he wasn't going to brag about his accomplishments. He intended to demonstrate to Max and Sebastian how wrong they were to underestimate him.

"Face it, Nat," Max continued. "You're not going to get the deal with Montgomery done. Silas is just leading you on. Which brings me to the reason I called. We heard from Lucas Smythe. He's willing to take a meeting."

Max's news infuriated Nathan. Sebastian had been eager to bring Smythe Industries into the fold for a couple years. Buying the family-run business would further diversify Case Consolidated Holdings' portfolio. It was the perfect move for his risk-averse brothers.

"Why now? A year ago he turned us down flat."

"He didn't say and it doesn't matter. Sebastian and I like Lucas's company. There's not as much risk involved."

Or as much reward. "All I need is six weeks to get the details ironed out." He left the specifics deliberately vague. "If you give me time, I can make this deal happen."

"This isn't about you." Max's voice hardened. "It's about what's best for Case Consolidated Holdings. Stop acting like a lone wolf and prove to us that you can put the company's best interests before your ego."

"That's what I'm doing."

The unfairness of the criticism hit Nathan hard. He'd always been the one on the outside. His mother's long-term affair with Brandon had robbed Nathan of any chance for a normal family life. After her death, when he'd been twelve, he'd gone to live with the Case family. Neither the wife Brandon had cheated on, nor her overprotective sons had been happy to share a roof with the living proof of Brandon's infidelity. Sebastian and Max were thirteen months apart, with Nathan a mere six months younger than Max. But while his brothers were as tight as twins, they shut out Nathan completely.

"It's hard to act like part of the team when I've been treated like the opposition."

Silence followed Nathan's statement. When Max spoke again, he sounded colder than ever. "We'll see you in the office tomorrow."

"Sure."

"I'll set up a meeting with Sebastian in the afternoon. You can bring us up-to-date then."

Without waiting for Nathan's answer, Max disconnected the call. Nathan muttered a string of curses and inserted a CD. While Dierks Bentley reminded him that good things happen, Nathan contemplated his situation. The last six months had been hell. He probably wouldn't have lasted this long if he didn't love a challenge so much.

Nathan rested his elbow against the door and propped his head on his hand. Unbidden, the sexy image of Emma wearing the black thong and matching strapless bra rose in his mind as he thought back to the night of Grant's party. Her skin had been like hot silk beneath his fingers as he'd stripped her underwear off. She was exactly the sort he went for, all sultry sophistication and flashing sable eyes.

Her brother, Cody, had been his best friend in college. The first time Nathan had laid eyes on her, she'd been sixteen. The four-year difference in their ages made her jailbait, but she'd stalked him, her curiosity fully engaged on her journey from girl to woman.

An attractive, cheeky brat, she'd worn red lipstick to draw attention to her lush mouth, batted her long lashes and flaunted her shapely golden body in a string bikini every chance she got. She would arch her back and lift her wet hair so the breeze would catch the damp strands.

Amused by her kittenish play, he'd let her practice her feminine wiles on him. Keeping his distance, however, grew increasingly difficult as she got bolder. Then came the afternoon she caught him alone in the kitchen. In an insanely short skirt and high heels, she'd strutted past him, plying his libido with her sassy smile.

If he'd caught wind of her intentions, he'd have been out of there fast, but he never dreamed that she'd back him against a counter and set her full, rosy mouth on a collision course with his lips. For two sluggish heartbeats he'd stared at her pretty face, long lashes painting ebony half moons on her flushed cheeks, and been tempted to teach her a lesson on the dangers of flirting with older men. Instead, rattled by her detrimental effect on his good judgment, he'd rebuffed her without much finesse, cut his visit short and hit the highway.

Twelve years later she was no longer forbidden fruit.

Three weeks ago, he'd had his first taste, and it left him hungry for more.

With an impatient, disgusted snort he shoved the provocative pictures away and focused on the problem at hand:

convincing Emma to marry him. Because he couldn't do the deal with her father and take control of Case Consolidated Holdings away from his half brothers unless he did.

Three

Emma sat in the middle of her walk-in closet. Surrounded by empty hangers and four plastic garbage bags filled with the last of her designer clothes, she fought an overwhelming sense of hopelessness. She needed to replace $35,000 and had about five weeks to do it. The amount staggered her.

Her cell phone rang.

"I was calling to invite you out to dinner," Addison said, her tone brisk. "Paul's taking the kids to basketball practice tonight so I've got a couple hours free."

Emma pictured her best friend sitting in her beautifully decorated home office, going over the details for whatever event she was organizing. For the last five years, Addison had been growing her party planning business, working long hours, setting goals and achieving them. With a tireless work ethic and an abundance of determination, she inspired Emma's entrepreneurial drive and at the same time made Emma feel guilty that she didn't work harder.

"I don't know if I can make it," Emma said, when what she

really meant to say is that she didn't know if she could afford it. Thanks to her father's actions a year ago, she'd gone from spendthrift to penny pincher. The transformation had been humbling, but she recognized that it had also been a good lesson to learn. "I've been going through my closet to see what I can sell."

"Are you crying?"

Emma shook her head and dashed the back of her hand against her damp cheek. "No."

"You sound like you are. Why don't you just let me lend you the money?"

"You and Paul can't afford to do that. And I wouldn't take it anyway. I've got to do this on my own." She'd never get her father to stop meddling if she didn't beat him at his own game.

"You aren't going to make enough money in five weeks by selling your clothes. Have you heard from the people running the art and design show?"

A couple months ago, Addison had badgered her into applying for a spot at a prestigious art and design show in Baton Rouge. Unsure how her work would be received, Emma's nerves had been tied up in knots. Yesterday, she'd been accepted.

"I'm in. But I don't have enough inventory to take to the show. Almost everything is consigned at Biella's." By her calculation, she had at least $50,000 tied up in unsold jewelry. Almost all of it decorated the cases in Biella's, Houston's most prestigious jeweler.

"So, go there and get it back. It's not as if they've sold more than five or six pieces in the last six months. I think the Baton Rouge show's your best bet."

"But can I make enough?" Emma dumped a garbage bag out onto the floor and began sliding hangers back into her clothes. "Daddy says I don't have the drive to succeed. Maybe he's right."

"He's not right. I know you can do this and, deep down, so do you."

Did she? Emma wasn't so sure. Being independent and financially responsible was hard work. And, right now, the enormity of the task before her made her want to crawl back into bed and pull the covers over her head.

"Besides," Addison continued. "Don't you want to see the look on your father's face when he realizes he has to turn your money over to you? It should be priceless."

Addison's enthusiasm bolstered Emma's sagging confidence. "What would I do without you?"

"Fortunately, you'll never have to know. Now, put on some Prada and get going."

An hour later, Emma stepped into Biella's, and paused just inside the glass doors. Fidgeting with her gold hoop earring, she scanned the large space. The exclusive downtown Houston jewelry store had been split into two parts. Diamonds and precious stone rings occupied one side, while necklaces, bracelets, watches and men's jewelry filled the cases on the other. Tones of cinnamon, gold and slate cradled the expensive collections. Copper-toned mirrors lined the walls behind the displays, reflecting the golden light from crystal chandeliers. Emma's feet sank into plush, dark gray carpet as she circled the room.

Little had changed since she'd honed her skills here as an apprentice goldsmith five years ago. The ambiance remained luxurious and elegant. The store owed as much of its success to the quality of the shopping experience as to the uniqueness of its merchandise.

An eager, smiling sales associate appeared ready to offer the knowledgeable assistance expected at Biella's. The redhead must be a new hire; otherwise, she'd recognize Emma and realize she wasn't a customer.

Emma approached the cases, drawing the sales consultant like a shark to fresh blood.

"Aren't these beautiful? A local artist does the work. Is there something you'd like to see up close?"

Thinking that she'd seen each and every piece up close already, Emma smiled at the clerk, appreciating her enthusiasm. "I was wondering if Thomas was around."

Thomas McMann was Biella's manager, and Emma's former boss. He'd been the one to propose the idea of consignment; Emma had hoped to sell the pieces outright. She understood his reluctance to take on so much inventory. Considering her lack of reputation, the price she'd assigned to each piece and the quality of the designs, he might not want to take a chance on such untraditional items.

"I'll see if he's available."

"Thanks."

While the girl disappeared into a back room, Emma counted the pieces in the display case to see if anything had been sold. Another two of the smaller pieces were missing. She breathed a sigh of relief. That meant another $3,000 in the bank.

It would make a little dent in the $35,000 she still had to put back. It was a huge amount to earn in five weeks, and she'd be lying if she said she wasn't daunted by the prospect, but failure meant she couldn't show her father and Nathan that she was a capable, independent woman who deserved to make her own choices about who she married and when.

Too bad she hadn't known about her father's plans for Nathan five months ago. She might not be in her current predicament. When her father first cut her off, it took her two months to go through a quarter of the money, and another thirty days before the reality of her troubles began sinking in.

She enjoyed designing and creating jewelry, but she'd never considered pursuing it as a career. It had been Addison who'd suggested that Emma could make enough money to keep herself afloat if she stuck with creating spectacular, one-of-a-kind pieces.

Unfortunately, setting herself up with the equipment and supplies she needed put another dent in the hundred thousand, and another thirty days melted away before she'd produced enough pieces to show the manager of Biella's what she could do. In the end, her hard work had paid off, and the first dollars she'd earned by selling what she'd made had given her a huge thrill.

"Hello, Emma," a soft nasal voice greeted. Tall and as thin as a cartoon rendering of Ichobod Crane, all elbows and skinny legs, Thomas McMann had a beak for a nose and incredible bedroom eyes framed by sumptuous eyelashes that belonged to a cover girl. "Did you see we sold three more pieces?"

"Three?" She rechecked. Sure enough. A little glow blossomed around her heart. She recognized it as confidence, something she'd been sorely lacking for the last eleven months. "That's terrific." She took the envelope he extended, resisting the urge to tear it open and see the size of the check.

"I hope you've brought us some new pieces."

"Actually, I was hoping to take these back." She pointed to the jewelry in the case. "I was invited to participate in an art and design show, and you have all my inventory."

"Oh. That's a problem." He looked at her somberly. "Your jewelry is really starting to sell, and we have two months left on our contract."

By that he meant he wasn't willing to give up the forty percent commission he took from each piece. Emma chewed on her lower lip.

"I'll return whatever doesn't sell at the show, and I'll design some new pieces as well."

A quarter-inch of glass and one man's stubbornness separated Emma from the glittering collection of jewelry she'd designed and crafted. Regaining possession of the necklaces, earrings and rings, embellished with diamonds and precious gems, was crucial to her plan.

"You can have whatever we haven't sold in two months." From his tone, he wasn't yielding. Thomas had always been a stickler for rules. It's what kept him in charge of Houston's top jewelry store for the last ten years, and why she'd left.

With her heart crushed to the size of a peanut, Emma blew out a breath and decided she'd better come up with plan B if she hoped to escape her father's marriage trap.

After leaving Biella's, she decided to stop by Case Consolidated Holdings and retrieve her earrings. If she hoped to have enough to sell at the show, she might have to sacrifice some of her personal favorites. She would need the earrings Nathan took.

Standing in the elevator, she watched the floor numbers light up one by one in the display panel beside the door. Her stomach gave a little lurch as the elevator slowed. She smoothed her simple beige silk dress, recognizing the nerves behind the gesture. More than nerves, she amended. Her heart thudded almost painfully in her chest. Panic better described it.

Until that moment, she'd forgotten that she'd stood him up for breakfast on New Year's Day. For the last few days she'd been so focused on her finances that she hadn't considered how annoyed he would be that she'd dodged him yet again. But how could she do otherwise when she'd almost given in and let him have his way with her a second time?

Just thinking about him, recalling what he'd said to her, the way he'd known exactly what would drive her crazy, she was hot and ready for a repeat performance of their one time together. Of course, there wouldn't be a repeat performance.

Emma entered the offices of Case Consolidated Holdings, immediately distracted from her mission by the original artwork hanging on the lobby walls. She stepped closer to one particular painting. Her eyes widened as she recognized the work of Julian Onderdonk, one of the most highly acclaimed Texas artists of the twentieth century.

He'd always been a favorite of Emma's because his work captured the subtle beauty of south Texas. She'd encouraged her father to purchase three of his paintings. He'd hung them in his study and often remarked that although they hadn't appealed to him when he'd first bought them, he came to appreciate the landscapes more every day.

"Can I help you?" the young woman at the reception desk inquired.

"In just a second." Emma moved on to the next painting.

Adrian Brewer, she mused. Painted in the late twenties. Emma admired the field of bluebonnets that drifted off into the expansive Texas horizon. Someone with a discerning eye shared her appreciation for early Texas artists. Who was the collector?

"Do you have an appointment?" the receptionist continued, her brisk tone disturbing Emma's reflective mood.

Art always had a powerful, soothing effect on her, and right now, she needed all the calm she could muster.

"I think she's here to see me," a familiar, masculine voice replied.

Nathan came to stand behind her right shoulder, close enough for her to feel the tension in his muscles. The hair on her arms lifted as if she stood in close proximity to a lightning strike. She froze, dazzled by the effect the man had on her.

How easy it would be to lean back against him and be enfolded in his arms, to let him take away her worries and drown her doubts in deep, drugging kisses. She inhaled his scent, a subtle blend of sandalwood soap and lavender shampoo, and recalled how his hair had felt between her fingers as she'd gripped him tight and encouraged him to feast on her. A groan collected in her throat. She eased her eyes shut to capture the memory and hold it tight.

"I always considered Julian Onderdonk the master of the bluebonnet," she said, grateful to hear the steadiness of her voice. Now if only she could count on the rest of her body to follow suit. "But after seeing Brewer's interpretation, I might have to change my mind."

"I wouldn't know anything about that," he retorted, clipping off the words with an impatience that banished her sensual daydreaming. "We buy purely for investment purposes."

Emma's eyes flashed open. She glanced up at his forbidding profile. He appeared preoccupied with the painting. Despite his grim expression, she detected a hint of softness in his lips. The gentleness vanished a second later as his flat, gray eyes slashed to her. Her pulse jerked.

Seizing her by the elbow, he drew her down the hall that stretched away from the receptionist's desk. The speech she'd prepared vanished at his touch. She was at a loss for words, wishing his impersonal grip didn't affect her so acutely.

The hall buzzed with activity, but Emma might have been blind and deaf for all the attention she paid. She couldn't concentrate on anything but Nathan and the annoyance radiating from him. Clearly, this had been a mistake.

He steered her into a huge office and abandoned her in the middle of the space. While he crossed to his desk, Emma glanced around. The walls held more artwork, this of a modern flavor, by artists whose work she didn't recognize. Half a dozen canvases sat propped against an end table. Yet as compelling as her curiosity about the art was, the man who owned it captivated her more.

Nathan stood before the wall of windows, hands clasped behind his back, and surveyed downtown Houston. The broad shoulders she'd caressed and clung to appeared no less intimidating encased in a charcoal-gray suit coat that matched his eyes. Sunlight stabbed through the window and drew forth the gold in his brown hair.

"To what do I owe the pleasure of this visit?" he asked.

It dawned on her that she'd used the excuse of retrieving her jewelry to see him again. "I came to collect my earrings."

"They're at my condo," he said. "We could go and pick them up."

Him and her alone in his condo would only lead to one thing. "I wouldn't want to put you out. Why don't you just bring them here tomorrow and I'll pick them up?"

"How about dinner tonight?" He countered.

Dinner with him sounded like a prelude to seduction. "How about breakfast tomorrow?"

For the first time since entering the room, he turned and faced her. "But if we started with dinner tonight, breakfast tomorrow will be inevitable."

The air sizzled with the power of his magnetism.

"I already have plans for dinner," she hedged as he advanced toward her. Emma backed up. If she didn't get out of here fast, he'd figure out how effortlessly he made her pulse race and her willpower waver. "How about we meet at nine tomorrow morning after my yoga class?" Preferably at a place where she couldn't be persuaded to take her clothes off. "I go to Carley's Café quite a bit."

"I don't think so." He shook his head. "You stood me up for breakfast once."

Emma doubted that he'd ever been stood up before. Cody had regaled her with enough of Nathan's conquests for her to recognize that he kept a woman around as long as it suited him to do so. *He* determined the length of the relationship, not the other way around.

She'd understood that three weeks ago when she'd left the party and gone to his penthouse condo overlooking downtown Houston. But that didn't mean she had to wait for him to grow tired of her, like all the other women who fell for his charms.

She shrugged. "Sorry about that. I had to get back to Houston right away."

"And the reason you didn't call and give me a heads-up?"

What could she say to that? "Because you don't take no for an answer."

"Funny," he murmured, his gaze trailing over her features, "that doesn't stop you from saying no to me."

With her heart thundering in her ears, she pressed her lips together to keep from spilling the truth. In the weeks since he'd taken her hard and fast against the front door of his condo, she'd been consumed with a crazy, irrational desire to see where dating him might lead. She'd been on the verge of returning his phone calls when her father had interfered and saved her from making a huge mistake.

"Until three weeks ago, you never gave me the chance," she said, immediately regretting both the statement and her aggrieved tone.

"I didn't realize you were that interested," he said, taking a step toward her.

His predatory intent induced Emma to take a step back. "I wasn't."

"No?"

Emma's pulse kicked up a notch, intensifying her need to retreat. When her back collided with something solid, she brushed aside her bangs in acute frustration. She'd misjudged her direction and missed the doorway. The wall kept her from escaping.

"Look." She tugged on her earring. "The night of Grant's party was nice."

"Nice?" he echoed, his tone neutral.

"It gave me closure."

He set his hand on the wall above her shoulder and leaned in. "Closure?"

"I wondered what…being with you would be like." She took a deep breath. "Now I know, and…"

His nostrils flared. "Let's see if I have this straight. You'd been curious what sex with me would be like? And now that you know, you're done with me?" Gray ice melted as heat blazed in his eyes. The rest of his expression remained frozen, but his searing, penetrating gaze heated places that would inspire her to surrender if she wasn't careful. "Well, let me set the record straight. I'm not done with you."

Traitorous impulses surged through Emma's body, undermining her resistance. She shoved Nathan's business deal with her father to the furthest reaches of her mind and gathered handfuls of his lapels, but before she could draw him closer, a tall brunette breezed into the office as if she belonged there.

"Nathan, I hope you're free to take me to lunch."

At the interruption, Emma's hands fell to her sides. Nathan shifted his gaze to follow the newcomer across his office and pushed away from the wall.

He smoothed his tie and straightened his suit coat. "Gabrielle, what are you doing here?"

"I've been craving Rolando's crab bisque all morning." The brunette set her purse on his desk and pulled out a compact, appearing oblivious to the charged atmosphere.

A wave of nausea pounded through Emma. She'd been a fool to think for even one second that she was the only woman Nathan was interested in. Scanning Gabrielle from her elegant haircut to her expensive shoes, Emma recognized that Nathan's taste in women ran to sophisticated, pampered brunettes with large bank accounts.

Nathan looked from her to Gabrielle and back again. Was he comparing his women? Who would he choose? The tense, pale girl in a simple beige dress or the accomplished flirt in the pencil-slim skirt, cowl-neck halter top and Manolo sandals?

"Nathan?" the brunette asked, sensing that she hadn't captured his complete attention. "Are you listening to me?" She turned around and spotted Emma. "Oh, is this your new assistant? I'm glad you finally listened to Sebastian and hired someone. Tell her to make reservations for us at Frey's."

"Gabrielle, this is Emma Montgomery. She is not my new assistant. Her father is Silas Montgomery of Montgomery Oil."

"Really?" Gabrielle turned the full power of her aquamarine eyes on Emma and perused her appearance with amusement. "Well, my daddy is chairman of the board and CEO of Parker Corporation."

What was this, battle of the spoiled heiresses? And adding to Emma's humiliation, Nathan had introduced her as if she was the daughter of a business associate instead of his... What? Lover? Girlfriend? Well, wasn't she?

Emma unclenched her jaw and forced her lips into a polite smile. "Nice to meet you, Gabrielle," she said, not meaning a single word. It was long past time to go. She slid sideways along the wall until she found the doorway, then practically fell on her behind when the gap appeared. Dodging the hand he reached out to her, she muttered, "Carly's Café at nine. Bring my earrings."

Beset by the sense that something had just gone very wrong, Nathan stepped into the hall. He watched Emma race away, fighting the urge to chase after her. His mood worsened when he reentered his office to find Gabrielle ensconced in one of his guest chairs, her skirt hiked up to show off her great legs.

"Ready to take me to lunch?" she demanded, her lower lip pushed out in a sulky expression she wore way too often. "I'm starving."

"See if Max is free."

"I don't want to have lunch with Max." Which meant they were arguing again. Gabrielle and Max had an on-again, off-again thing going. Nathan didn't understand it. There were plenty of women in Houston eager to help a guy scratch an itch. Why did Max put up with Gabrielle's demands and temper? "I want to have lunch with *you*."

She only wanted his company because she thought it bugged his brother. It didn't.

"I don't have time. I'll give Max a call for you."

"I'll bet you would have gone if she'd asked you." Gabrielle wasn't ready to give up. She leaned forward, running her hand along her shin to draw attention to her best asset. "What's up with her, anyway? And where the hell did she get that dress? I would expect someone with her kind of money to have better taste in clothes."

"I thought she looked fine."

Indeed, the dress's scoop neck had shown off a hint of cleavage and the hundred tiny buttons running from neckline to hem had awakened an urgent desire in Nathan to unfasten every one, or give up and rip the garment right off her. Arousal lashed him like an unexpected storm. He dropped into his leather desk chair to keep Gabrielle from noticing.

Picking up the phone, he dialed. "Max, Gabrielle wants to have lunch with you."

She squawked in protest and got to her feet.

"Great," he continued. "I'll let her know."

"He's on his way." Nathan replaced the phone.

Hoping this would be the last time he'd see Gabrielle at Case Consolidated Holdings, Nathan flashed her a broad grin. Maybe Max would send her packing, the way he had sent the last dozen packing, with a full stomach and a firm, noncommittal goodbye. Gabrielle had been bragging of late that she'd succeeded in enticing the elusive Max Case from his bachelor ways. Nathan almost felt sorry for her.

The next morning, a heated discussion was taking place in Sebastian's big corner office.

"I've looked at Smythe's numbers. It seems like a pretty solid deal," Sebastian said, as cool and unflappable as Max was hot and animated. "Which means we're not going to be able to do the deal with Montgomery Oil."

Nathan tapped his pen on his yellow legal pad to keep his temper from flaring again. "I put in a call to a buddy of mine in Chicago in investment banking. He's got the inside scoop on Smythe. The guy is not going to sell."

"And we're just supposed to believe your *buddy?*" Max demanded.

Nathan shrugged. "It doesn't change the fact that if Smythe does sell, we won't have nearly the potential for profit as we would if we did the deal with Montgomery." His temper slipped. "And if you two would stop acting like a couple of old women, you might understand the value in taking a little risk."

"Don't lecture us about taking risks," Max shot back. "You're nothing but a hotshot who wouldn't be here if Dad—"

Max had always doled out his criticism with boisterous, taunting directness. Sebastian chose a quieter, deadlier approach.

"I'm sure Nathan understands his position in this company."

Yeah, Nathan understood his position all right. He was an outsider. It didn't matter that he bore their last name. His mother had been Brandon Case's mistress. He wasn't their "legitimate" brother, and they resented that they'd been forced to share their father with him. And now their company.

"Don't give up on the deal with Montgomery," Nathan said, letting the subtle and not so subtle jabs slide off him. He would get nowhere if he continued to agitate his brothers. "I told you I have a couple things to iron out in order to get things finalized. Give me a few more weeks. You owe me that."

"Forget it, Nat," Max said. "You took your shot and lost."

I didn't lose. "Don't be an idiot. You've seen the numbers.

The technology is poised to explode, and if we get in on the ground floor, we'll make a killing." He leaned forward. "Look, I get that you're angry that Dad didn't consult you when he brought me on board. You want me gone, but that's not going to happen. So you might as well quit playing games."

"What's that supposed to mean?" Sebastian exchanged a look with Max.

"Ever since we were kids you two have ganged up against me. I get why. I was the illegitimate one. The proof that your father had cheated on your mother. Well, that was a long time ago. My mother's been dead twenty years. Don't you two think it's time you let it go?"

Both his brothers looked surprised by his vehemence. They turned to each other and another of those nonverbal exchanges passed between them. Nathan hated how their closeness shut him out. It renewed his determination to take control of the company away from them.

"What do we really know about this technology you want to invest in?" Max grumbled, his body language and expression broadcasting his skepticism. "We're out of our depth here."

Nathan stared at his brother. "I'm not."

"Well, excuse me if I'm having trouble taking your word on this."

Sebastian silenced his younger brother with a sharp gesture. "Nathan has given us solid numbers on this, Max. Until this thing came up with Smythe, we agreed to give him a chance to approach Montgomery about their joint venture. Silas hasn't made a decision. I think we should at least give Nathan until the middle of February. If he's right about Lucas, we can afford to wait."

"I never thought you'd be up for this kind of risk, Sebastian," Max said, his eyes narrowing. "That sort of gambling is better left to the experts." A great deal of sarcasm went into the last word.

Nathan sidestepped the urge to react to his brother's taunt, but it rankled. He didn't have an MBA or their business credentials, but he'd made a hell of a lot of money on his ability to research up-and-coming companies and glimpse their potential.

"Why don't you discuss it?" Nathan glanced at his watch. He was going to be late if he didn't get going right away. "I've got a breakfast meeting. Let me know what you decide."

Leaving his brothers to make their decision, Nathan grabbed his coat and headed out. Carley's Café was a three-block walk, and he let the chilly winter air cool his anger as he strode along the sidewalk. For the first time in months— maybe even years—he had a project he could sink his teeth into. He would not give up because of his brothers' timidity and lack of imagination.

He hadn't completely banished his ill humor by the time he pushed into the tiny restaurant, but his pulse kicked up in anticipation of seeing Emma again. At this hour, there was only one table available. He stripped off his coat, ordered coffee and settled down to wait.

When the waitress offered to refill his cup a second time, he glanced at his watch. Where the hell was she? It was already half an hour past the time she'd promised to meet him. He tossed money on the table and donned his coat.

Cody had given him her address weeks ago. After their encounter at his condo, he'd considered sending flowers, a balloon bouquet, something foolish and romantic. The impulse disturbed him. He wasn't the foolish, romantic sort. In the end, he hadn't done anything, and after she'd ignored his phone calls, he was damn glad.

Nathan walked the five blocks to her building and slipped in without having to warn her of his arrival, thanks to the woman who exited the secure front door just as he arrived. He crossed the newly remodeled lobby to the refurbished freight elevator, imagining Emma's shock when she answered the door.

On the fourth floor, Nathan found Emma's unit and rang her doorbell. When no one answered, he tried again. While he considered that she might refuse to let him in, he doubted that she would be hiding inside, pretending she wasn't home. He tried the doorknob and, to his surprise, found the door unlocked. Entering the unit, he called Emma's name.

The only noise that reached his ears sounded like someone being violently sick.

He crossed the living room, absently inventorying the size of the place and the abundance of renovation projects left incomplete, and headed down a narrow hallway, following a hunch. At the end of the hall he hit pay dirt. What he found dismayed him.

Someone had taken a sledgehammer to the master bathroom and completely gutted the space. The walls and ceiling had been stripped down to the studs, exposing the wiring and plumbing. Where the shower should have been, he noticed rotten wood, mottled with black stains. The only fixtures in the entire room still intact were the sink and the toilet. And that's where he found Emma, hunched over the bowl, her eyes wide and incredulous in a face the color of chalk. She wiped her mouth with the back of her hand.

"Nathan?" She closed her eyes, and her face twisted into an expression of agony. "What are you doing here?"

Before he could answer she had leaned over the toilet and heaved. Concern for her overrode his earlier irritation. He knelt beside her and soothed his hand over her shoulder, buffeted by an all-too-familiar feeling of helplessness. How many times had he sat by his mom after her chemo treatments and struggled with the frustration of not being able to help her?

"I came to see why you stood me up again."

"And now that you've seen why I couldn't make it, you can be on your merry way."

Her rejection didn't faze him at all. "And leave you like this? Not likely." He cast around the dismantled space looking for a towel. "I'll be right back."

He retraced his steps down the hall and entered her tiny kitchen. The ancient cabinets and outdated appliances indicated that her renovation project hadn't gone far. That was probably for the best if her bathroom was any indication of how badly the remodeling was going. He found a kitchen towel and ran it under the cold water. He squeezed out the excess and returned to the bathroom. Emma sat where he'd left her.

"Here, this should make you feel a little better." He applied the wet towel to her cheeks and forehead, peering at her in concern. "What were you celebrating?"

She had enough strength to glare at him, but not enough to fight his ministrations. "This is not a hangover. It's food poisoning. Go away."

He sat down on the floor beside her, not caring that the torn-up flooring would ruin his expensive suit. It bothered him to see her in these sorts of surroundings. No wonder her father wanted her married off. She obviously needed someone to take care of her.

Something reached through his concern and stunned him with its possibility.

"Is there something else?" she demanded. "Because I'm not really feeling up to entertaining you."

He pushed a lock of hair behind her ear. "Are you sure this is food poisoning?"

"What else could it be?" Her brows came together.

"Well, it's been almost a month since we were together." His voice trailed off as he scrutinized her expression.

Emma eyed him through her long bangs. "And?"

"Are you pregnant?"

Four

Pregnant? Emma's queasiness now originated from a whole new source. Foreboding surfaced like a rash. Her focus narrowed to the irritation of a persistent itch that wouldn't go away, no matter how long or hard she scratched.

She had food poisoning. Nothing more.

"We used protection," she reminded him, her voice a noon shadow.

"It's not one hundred percent effective."

Oh, and wouldn't he love that. He'd have even more leverage to get her to marry him if she turned out to be pregnant. Closing the door on her doubts, she glared at him. "Go away."

"I'm not leaving you like this," he said. "I'm going to get you some water."

"No, please." While she acknowledged that her body could use some fluids right now, she didn't want Nathan around while she felt so weak and helpless. It was just too easy to lean on him, let him handle things. And before she knew it, he would have her agreeing to marry him. "Just leave me in peace."

"You can't afford to get dehydrated."

She hid her face in her arms. "I really don't think I could keep anything down."

Although exhausted by her rough morning, Emma suspected that Nathan wouldn't leave until she proved that she could take care of herself. Hoping her stomach could take it, she began pushing to her feet. Before she could stand upright, Nathan bent down and swept her into his arms. Too shocked and too weak to protest, Emma gripped his shoulders for stability. The short walk to her bedroom reminded her how many times in the last three weeks she wished she'd stayed at his condo that night. Would he have carried her to bed like this?

He set her on her feet and kept one arm around her waist as he swept the covers aside. "For the last month I've been looking forward to getting you into bed," he said, the grim, unyielding businessman morphing into a handsome snake charmer. "But this isn't exactly what I had in mind."

She quashed the amusement his comment produced. Gorgeous, cheeky and way too sexy for his own good, she resented that he seemed to know exactly what to say to make her forget that she'd been up and sitting within arms' reach of the toilet since just before five o'clock when she had been overcome by nausea.

"I'm in no condition to flirt with you," she told him as a wave of dizziness hit her.

His wry grin faded as he pulled the covers over her. "Can I get you anything?"

She clutched the edge of her comforter and stared up at him. Her stomach flipped in a way that had nothing to do with food poisoning.

"No. I'll be fine." She probably should thank him for taking care of her, but he'd entered her home uninvited and had stumbled upon her in the most humiliating of moments. No, she didn't have to feel one bit grateful. If only he'd go. "I'm going to sleep for a while."

She shut her eyes, to block out the concern tangling with humor in his dark gray eyes, and hoped he'd take the hint. Retreating footsteps told her that he'd left her room, but she couldn't relax while sounds of him moving around the loft reached her ears. He returned to the bedroom and placed something on the nightstand beside her. She spied a glass of water within easy reach just as she heard the front door to the apartment open and shut. Although every muscle protested, she slipped out of bed and slowly crossed the living room to slide the dead bolt home.

Her legs shook with the effort of retracing her steps across the expansive space. She caught at the door frame leading to her bedroom as her vision darkened. Gulping air, she shuffled five steps and dropped into bed, pulling the covers over her. As her body went limp, sleep claimed her at last.

When she woke late that afternoon, the food poisoning seemed to have run its course. Feeling weak and shaky from low blood sugar and lack of water, Emma swung her legs out of bed and sat up. While her head swam, her stomach barely reacted at all. With a faint, relieved smile, she headed for the kitchen. A piece of toast and a cup of herbal tea sounded like heaven. The smell of cooking brought her up short.

Emma pushed her sleep-tossed hair out of her eyes and gaped at the man standing in her kitchen. Nathan had replaced his expensive business suit with thigh-hugging jeans and a long-sleeved blue sweater that emphasized the capable strength of his torso.

His gaze swept over her. She'd caught a glimpse of herself as she'd passed her dresser mirror. It wasn't pretty. She waited for his expression to reflect disappointment. But as he perused her ancient but comfortable cotton pajama bottoms and lingered over the fact that she wasn't wearing a bra beneath her equally worn T-shirt, only appreciation altered the curve of his lips.

Her nipples tightened, driving a spike of longing straight to her core. She crossed her arms over her chest a fraction too late. His smug grin confirmed that her body's involuntary response hadn't gone unnoticed. Why couldn't he disapprove of her appearance just this once? It would give her a firm base to build resentment on. Instead, she felt all mushy and weak-kneed.

"I see you're up." He stirred something in a pot on the stove, something that smelled heavenly. "Feeling better?"

"You left."

"I went out and bought some supplies. I figured you'd be hungry when you woke up."

"I locked the door."

"I anticipated that and took your keys with me."

Damn the man for having all the answers. She retreated to her room to put on a robe and comb her hair. Using the water he'd left beside her bed, she brushed her teeth. A quick rinse with mouthwash, and she returned to sit on a stool at her breakfast bar and scowl at him.

"You certainly have made yourself at home," she groused. "I don't recall issuing you an invitation to dinner."

"You were in no shape to issue any sort of invitation." His slow smile increased the room's temperature. "But I've always had a knack for anticipating a woman's needs." He nudged a teacup toward her. "It's peppermint. Good for nausea."

Wondering how he'd know something like that, Emma sipped the tea. "Are you sure it was my needs you were anticipating and not yours?"

"I assure you, I thought only of you."

Skepticism rumbled in her throat. Emma nodded toward the stove. "What are you cooking?"

"Chicken soup. My mother's recipe."

Now this was too much. "From scratch?"

"That's the only way. Would you like to try some?"

"How could I resist?"

Nathan dished up two bowls and pushed a plate of crackers toward her. Emma inhaled the soup's aroma and her stomach growled impatiently. The first spoonful of smooth chicken broth slid across her tongue, stimulating her taste buds with cilantro, lime and a hint of onion.

"This is delicious."

"It's not bothering your stomach?"

"Not at all. What a relief."

Nathan finished his soup and set his bowl in her sink.

"Are you feeling strong enough to tell me what happened to your bathroom?"

"I had a leak in the shower."

"Looks like overkill for a leak."

"The plumber I hired found mold. I had him rip everything out so we could see how bad it was."

Her explanation made him hiss in exasperation. "How long has it been like this?"

"A couple weeks."

"You need to get this taken care of."

She resented his assumption that she needed him to point that out to her. "It's the holidays and everyone I called is busy until the end of January."

"Mold is dangerous. You can't stay here."

"I've been living here for a year. I can survive another month." Besides, she had no place to go.

"It's dangerous," he repeated. "Why didn't you check into a hotel?"

"I can't afford to."

"Why not?"

It was time to explain what was really going on. "Last February, Daddy cut me off from my trust fund and gave me a hundred thousand to live on for the year."

"Why a hundred thousand?"

Emma grimaced. "It's what I spent on shoes the year before." Seeing the grin tugging at Nathan's lips, she rushed on. "New Year's Eve, Daddy and I made a deal. If I replace the hundred thousand in my account by Valentine's Day, he's promised to sign over my money and I don't have to marry you." She loaded the last bit with enough satisfaction to wipe the amusement off his face, but her smug words had no effect.

"Let me guess how much you have to replace." He cocked an eyebrow. "Fifty thousand?"

"Thirty-five."

His smirk made her blood boil. Why had she told him about the deal with her father? Over the years, Cody had probably regaled Nathan with assorted tales of her spending sprees. But she wasn't the same frivolous girl she'd been ten months ago. She'd learned to budget. She'd spent long hours designing and making her jewelry. And she'd figured out the best way to market it.

"The earrings you took. I need them back."

"Are you planning on selling them?"

"As a matter of fact, I am. I've started a business. I design fine jewelry. Expensive, original, one-of-a-kind pieces."

Except her father didn't take what she did seriously. And from the look on Nathan's face, he didn't, either. The harder she worked, the more she wanted her father to recognize her talent. How could you claim to love someone and not get them? Replacing the hundred thousand had become as much about proving to her father that she was great at something as it was about getting her trust fund back.

"I'm going to put the money back in my account," she said.

Instead of appearing concerned that she might succeed, he shrugged. "You don't seriously think you can do that in five weeks."

He sounded just like her father. When he looked at her, he saw only failure. Wouldn't he be surprised when she demonstrated just how capable she was? "I have a big art and design show coming up. I'll make more than enough money."

Naturally, she left out the part about lacking inventory to sell and how buying the supplies she needed would mean dipping back into the account she was trying desperately to replenish.

"I'm sure you make very nice jewelry," he told her in a patronizing manner that made her grind her teeth. "But you don't seriously expect to make enough money at some craft fair."

"I can do it," she declared, annoyed with him for echoing her own doubts about her plan. "You'll see."

"In the meantime, you can move into my condo while your bathroom is fixed."

"Move…" In with him? Emma stared at Nathan. "Absolutely not."

"Well, I'm not going to let you stay here," Nathan retorted, brisk with impatience. "I'll find someone to come in and take care of the mold and get your bathroom working again. It shouldn't take more than a couple weeks. In the meantime, you can stay with me."

"I'd appreciate your help with a contractor, but I'm not staying with you."

A sly smile softened his sculpted lips. "Afraid you might like it too much to leave?"

His question aroused memories of New Year's Eve, reminding her how close she had come to succumbing to his charms. She began to tingle beneath the molten steel in his eyes. As he watched her struggle for an answer, his eyebrows lifted.

"I'm not afraid," she retorted, crossing her arms over her chest. Oh, but she was.

She craved his hands on her, his mouth claiming hers, and it robbed her of sanity, just as his knowing grin stole her breath. What would it be like to fall asleep sheltered by his arms each night? To be awakened every morning by the sensual slide of his naked muscles against her skin? Just thinking about it nudged her into the realm of an addict. If she let herself fall into his trap of seduction, she'd never be able to escape.

He shook his head. "I think you are." His eyebrows dropped back into their customary position, his lips curved ironically and he peered at her askance. "What are you fighting so hard to prove? You and I both know you aren't the independent sort. You'll be happier once you're married and have someone to take care of you. Your father knows it, too. That's why he's so determined to see you settled."

Growing up, whenever Emma had played with her dolls, she imagined they were falling in love and living happily ever after. By eighteen, she had her life all planned out, something her college friends had teased her about incessantly. She would get married shortly after college, to a man who adored her. She would be pregnant with her first child three years later. Between socializing with her friends, dinner parties with her husband's business associates and charity events, she would be blissfully happy. But her ex-fiancé, Jackson, had spoiled her innocent dreams.

Having to guard herself so vigilantly against making another mistake in love while longing to let go and take the plunge was a tug-of-war that took its toll. And the longer she fought, the more resistant she became to the trust she needed in order to let herself fall in love. Surrendering to her emotions became a thing of her past. Until Nathan Case had reentered her life.

"I thought you understood that I'm not going to marry you because of some business deal." Finishing the last of the tea, she leaned over the breakfast bar and put the cup in the sink.

She fixed a steady gaze on Nathan as he moved out of the kitchen in her direction. "Someday I will marry, but on my terms—not my father's."

He stepped between her thighs and caught her face in his hands. The instant he entered her space, her senses filled with the scent and power of him and her bones melted.

"Marry me," he coaxed. "You won't regret it."

Her heart jolted as he regarded her somberly. With his proposal ringing in her ears, she gripped his sweater, and then hesitated, uncertain as to whether to push him away or pull him close.

"Nathan." His name left her lips in a low plea for him to stop, to continue. He swooped into her moment of indecision and took charge. Dipping his head, he grazed her lips with his. The action froze them both.

"Sweet heaven," he murmured.

An astonishing tumult fluttered in her breast as he dragged his mouth over hers, absorbing her breath, teasing her with the promise of passion. Emma lost herself in the pliant caress of his lips. A sigh broke from her throat.

Then shock dimmed, replaced by a sweet wildness. Her heart plummeted to her toes only to rebound into glorious rapturous flight. She opened to the questing fire of his tongue, and the whirling increased, forcing her to hang on for dear life.

Hard arms came around her, binding her so close to his chest, their hearts beat in time. She wanted control of her body. She wanted control of her mind. Emma got neither. Nathan's kiss seduced reason from her world.

She slid her fingers into his hair, savoring the caress of softness against her skin. His hands moved slowly down her spine, unleashing an earthquake of trembling. Every nerve ending came alive with rollicking, shivering delight. Behind her eyes, stars sparkled.

No one but Nathan made her feel like this.

So much.

So fast.

Buffeted by emotion too strong to resist, she watched dry land recede. Protecting herself in a harbor might be dull, but she wouldn't drown in heartache. But it was too late to turn back. She was adrift in a stormy sea of passion. She would have to trust Nathan to guide her safely home.

Releasing fear, disregarding the promises she'd made to herself, Emma locked her legs around his thighs, holding him close with her soles pressed against his calves. His kisses became more demanding. With her arms wrapped around his neck, she surrendered to his strength, needing his mastery, yielding to his passion.

By pressing his hips toward hers, he made her aware of his arousal. His need. The hard length of him nudged against her core, already lava-hot. Her blood pooled and pulsed between her thighs, awakening a hunger that could only be slaked by this man.

He swept scorching caresses up her sides, edging the fabric of her T-shirt up. She moaned as he swallowed her breasts in his palms, fingers gliding along her skin, measuring and caressing, driving her crazy as he circled her hardening nipples.

"Emma." He rasped her name, half entreaty, half demand. "Look at me."

Losing herself in the sensations raging through her would be a lot easier with her eyes closed. She could concentrate on his deft touch and pretend that Nathan caressed her with emotion as well as passion.

"I don't think that's a good idea."

"You can't run from this."

No, but she could hide.

A sigh slipped from between her lips as she opened her eyes and met his gaze. The expression on his face warned her that he intended to devour her. "I'm not going anywhere."

She couldn't. Her longing for him trapped her as effectively as the steel bars of a cage.

"Good."

When he ducked his head, Emma watched him swirl his tongue around her breast and she arched her back, pushing into the caress, as aroused by his touch as she was by the sight of what he was doing to her.

His hand slipped beneath the elastic of her pajama bottoms. Her breath emerged in a frustrated groan as his fingertips dipped between her thighs and stopped short of where she wanted him. She pressed herself against him, gyrating in a manner that demonstrated her need.

"Touch me," she pleaded, long past caring how smug he might be at the depth of her desperation. All pride and every hesitation flew out the window whenever he touched her.

She moaned as he obliged, her body shuddering as his clever fingers slid against her.

"Oh baby, that's it," he crooned before claiming her mouth again. "Let go."

His mouth claimed hers again. She rocked against his hand, while urgent, encouraging sounds emanated from her throat. Her muscles tensed as she mindlessly sought the pleasure that danced just out of reach. Every sense was trained on the man making her body sing. She filled her lungs with the scent of his cologne. He tasted like chicken soup and peppermint tea, comforting and soothing. His deep voice, murmuring erotic suggestions in her ear, drove her crazy and made her want to laugh with joy at the same time.

And then there was the pleasure. The indescribable, building pressure that threatened to take her head off when it blew. She panted, her breath coming in irregular gasps. With his name on her lips, she climaxed. His mouth crashed down on hers, taking her cries into him, capturing her pleasure as his own.

As the fog cleared from her brain, Emma tugged on his

sweater, needing the feel of his skin. He obliged her by sweeping it off. She explored the ridges and texture of his gorgeous torso. A contented purr rumbled out of her. She craved the feel of his bare chest sliding over the hot skin of her breasts.

Nathan was of the same mind, because he murmured, "Naked." His fingers flexed into her hips, the bite causing a spike in her urgency. "I need you naked."

"Okay."

Something stirred in the depths of Nathan's eyes, swirling like smoke. Satisfaction? Triumph?

While nerves fluttered in her midsection, Emma bit down on her lower lip. A low noise rumbled in his chest. Nathan bent his head, his tongue soothing the dents left behind by her teeth. Breath catching, she tangled with him in a sexy kiss that reawakened her appetite, and then groaned in protest when he tore his mouth from hers.

"This is going to happen fast," he said, his voice dark and gritty. "Do you want it here or in bed?"

"Bed," she whispered, sliding off the stool, only to find that her legs could barely support her.

Five

Satisfaction exploded in Nathan's chest as Emma swayed across the meager inches between them, her fingers fanning against his bare chest. He liked how it was between them. Hot, sweaty, all-consuming and sexual. Easy to succumb. Mindless in its intensity. A feast for the senses.

He wrapped his arm around her waist and bent to sweep her feet off the floor. She gasped as he lifted her, and her fingers dug into his shoulders. Her liquid-chocolate eyes sought his. Despite her earlier passion, she looked somewhat uncertain. Needing to seal the deal before she had second thoughts, he turned toward the bedroom.

He'd taken one step when her doorbell rang. Nathan saw immediately that the interruption had startled the sensual glow from her eyes. A frown appeared between her finely arched eyebrows as she looked at the door. She bit down on her lower lip, even white teeth contrasting against the passion-bruised darkness of her mouth. He growled.

"Ignore it," he said, his long strides carrying him away from the sound of the intruder.

"I can't."

He was within ten feet of the bedroom door when the pounding began, followed by a feminine shout.

"Emma, are you all right? I've been calling all day. Emma, can you hear me?"

"It's Addison. I missed our yoga class this morning and never called her." Emma began to squirm. "Put me down."

Her words splashed cold water over his ardor. Muttering curses, Nathan set her back on her feet and watched in disgust as she raced to the door without so much as a backward glance. He retraced his steps at a much slower pace and scooped his sweater off the floor.

"Have you been home all day? I've been worried sick." A tall, thin woman, dressed casually in ultraexpensive designer clothes and radiating intense concern, burst through the door Emma opened. With a long, narrow face, aristocratic nose and sharp cheekbones, she was elegantly beautiful. Her long, straight red hair blew back from her shoulders as she spun to give Emma a thorough once-over. As concern for Emma faded, her voice became as voluptuous as her body was angular. "I suppose you were working and turned off the phone."

"I'm sorry I didn't call you, I spent most of the day in bed." Emma's gaze flickered in Nathan's direction.

He offered her his most salacious grin. Even across the room he could see the color that flooded her cheeks.

"Were you sick?" Addison glanced over her shoulder in the direction of her friend's gaze and her perfect cupid-bow lips dropped open at the sight of Nathan standing half-naked beside the breakfast bar.

He let the woman's pale blue eyes drink their fill of his bare chest and obvious arousal before he casually slipped the blue sweater over his head. Sliding it into place, he strode forward and held out his hand.

"Hello, I don't think we've met. I'm—"

"Nathan Case," she finished for him, extending her hand. "Addison Clements."

Either she was one of those women who didn't believe a firm grip was feminine, or her astonishment at finding a half-naked man in her friend's loft left her dazed, because she scarcely put any effort into the handshake.

"He stopped by to check on me, too. We were supposed to have breakfast this morning, and I missed our meeting because I was sick." Emma emphasized the last three words, to deflect her friend's obvious curiosity. "I think I had food poisoning from dinner last night. Were you okay? I meant to call, but I felt so awful."

"I've been fine," Addison murmured, unable to take her eyes off Nathan.

He could see more than curiosity in her almond-shaped eyes. He glimpsed speculation as well.

"I'm sure you ladies have a lot to talk about," he said, catching Emma's hand and dropping a kiss into her palm. She quivered. "I'll be going. Nice to meet you, Addison."

Addison walked toward the kitchen, giving them some privacy. Emma followed Nathan to the door. Emotions whirled and churned through her as she tried to process what had almost happened again with him. How had he overridden her better judgment so easily?

Before she realized his intention, his hand slid along her hip, pulling her firmly against him. He dipped his head and claimed her lips, drowning her protests in a sensual assault. Her spine remained rigid for all of two heartbeats. Wrapped in the spicy scent of his cologne and the soothing warmth of his skin, she sagged against his chest.

With her surrender complete, Nathan eased his mouth

from hers. While his hands spanned her back, thumbs moving rhythmically, he spent a long moment nuzzling her temple.

"I'm going to send movers for your stuff tomorrow."

Despite his unsteady breathing, he sounded unaffected by the kiss. Humiliated that she'd fallen back into his arms so quickly, she applied pressure to his chest. He pulled back but was slow to release her. Her heart hammered against her ribs as his hands eased down her back and over her hips.

"I already told you I'm not going anywhere." She flinched at the breathy, disturbed timbre of her voice. It was bad enough that she dropped her guard any time he touched her—did she have to broadcast it?

"You have mold in your bathroom. And who knows where else. It's dangerous for you to stay here."

"That might be true but—"

"I have a perfectly nice condo and you can have your very own room." He smirked at her, undaunted by her temper or her refusal to cooperate with him. "Unless, of course, you'd like to share a bedroom with me."

She clenched her teeth to suppress a sarcastic retort. Why rise to the bait when that seemed to be exactly what he wanted? "I'm not moving in with you."

"She can stay with Paul and me," Addison called from the kitchen, where she'd obviously been eavesdropping.

Emma heaved a sigh, disliking the way they were ganging up on her. "You don't have room."

"The boys can share for a couple weeks. It won't kill them."

"The way those two argue, it might. Besides, I need to get ready for the show and that means I have to be here to work, so moving out doesn't make sense." Her shoulders felt as if a thirty-pound weight had been draped across them. "I'll be fine."

"You can move your worktable and equipment into my spare room," Nathan said.

Their combined logic beat her back like a phalanx of soldiers intent on conquering enemy territory. "Why don't we wait and see what your contractor has to say about the mold?"

"And if he recommends that you move out?" Nathan prompted.

"Then I will."

"That's my girl."

Setting his hand beneath her chin, Nathan tipped her head up. What she saw in his wolf-gray eyes set her heart to pounding. A slow, sly smile curved his sculpted lips.

She sucked in a sharp breath. "I'm not your girl."

"Sure you are." He kissed her on the nose. "You just don't want to admit it yet."

With that parting shot, he set her free and turned to go. His possessive declaration annoyed her. She didn't belong to him. Not yet. Not as long as she kept him at arm's length.

She leaned her hot cheek against the doorframe and watched his progress down the hall, appreciating the way his broad shoulders tapered to a narrow waist and his worn jeans cupped his perfect butt. Unruly cravings surged anew. Her fingers tightened on the door. Addison's arrival had been a lucky break. Convincing Nathan that she wasn't going to fall for him would have been that much harder after he completely transformed her into a moaning, writhing hedonist.

Catching her watching him, he flashed a cocky grin before stepping onto the elevator. Furious with herself for staring after him like some infatuated idiot, Emma slammed the door shut.

"Well, I obviously interrupted something," Addison said from the kitchen. She snagged a bottle of water from Emma's refrigerator. "Sorry."

Addison didn't look anything of the sort. Emma made a face at her.

"You didn't interrupt anything."

"Nice try," Addison said. "But he wasn't wearing a shirt and your eyes are wearing that half-dreamy, half-hungry look you get when you talk about him."

"I do not."

"Oh please. You've had a thing for him since you were sixteen. And from the way he kissed you just now, the feeling's obviously mutual."

Emma ignored her friend's last remark. "He's only interested in me because he wants to do a deal with my dad."

"I doubt that's the only reason." Addison waved away the beginnings of Emma's protests. "Yes, I know, your father is a controlling nightmare, blah, blah, blah. But you keep saying you want to fall in love and get married, yet you're so afraid that every man's going to be another Jackson that you don't give anyone a chance."

"Did you ever think that maybe I had good reason to keep my guard up?" Addison's lecture slid like needles into her insecurities. Irritated, she decided her oh-so-smart friend needed a better grasp on the situation. "And, for your information, Dad made marrying me a condition of the deal between his company and Nathan's."

Addison remained unfazed by Emma's revelation. "From everything I've heard about Nathan Case, he isn't anything like Jackson," she said, her tone calm and confident. "He's not going to marry you to get on your dad's good side."

"It's the only reason he wants to marry me," she shot back.

"So, say no."

"I'm trying."

Addison's lips twitched. "Not very hard. I obviously interrupted something pretty hot and heavy between you two."

Emma dropped her forehead onto the breakfast bar with a groan. "It's as if I spontaneously combust every time he touches me." Her head came up. "But that's not enough. I need more than sex." Incredible. Fabulous. Mind-blowing sex.

"Are you sure? Seems like you haven't been getting a lot of great sex lately. Or any sex, for that matter."

Emma didn't want to think about great sex with Nathan. Because if she thought about great sex, or any sort of sex with the man, she was going to have a hard time not having it with him again.

"Positive."

"I saw the way you two looked at each other," Addison said. "Maybe this thing between you two could lead to something more. It might be worth the risk. You haven't taken many of those lately, either."

Could it? Temptation tangled her resolve with a whole host of possibilities and left her adrift in confusion. She claimed that she wanted to fall in love and get married, but wasn't that all about taking chances? Was Addison right? Did she use her father's meddling in her life and her past naiveté as far as Jackson was concerned to guard her heart? Was she her own worst enemy when it came to finding someone to spend the rest of her life with?

After a moment, Emma shook her head. "Nathan approaches marriage like a business arrangement. I want to marry a man I love and who loves me in return. I want the fairy-tale ending. What's wrong with that?"

"Women get rescued in fairy tales," Addison pointed out. "Cinderella, Snow White, Rapunzel, Sleeping Beauty. All rescued. I thought you were trying to prove to your father that you can take care of yourself."

"All the more reason not to get involved with Nathan. He thinks exactly the way my father does. That I need him to look after me." She huffed. "And I don't."

Into the silence that fell between them, Addison added one last bit of advice. "I hope whatever decision you make, you don't regret it."

On that, Emma wholeheartedly agreed.

* * *

True to his word, Nathan sent a contractor to her loft the following morning. The stocky man had a brisk way of talking and a competent air as he inspected her bathroom.

"No wonder you've got problems." He wore a disgruntled expression as he surveyed the plumbing job done by the previous owners. "I've never seen such poor workmanship."

Emma set her hands on her hips. "But you can fix it?"

"Sure, but first we've got to get rid of this black mold," the contractor explained. "It's the most toxic variety there is. Can cause headaches, dizziness, difficulty concentrating. Not to mention runny nose and itchy eyes, and it could irritate or damage your lungs. I'd recommend that you vacate until we can get the problem taken care of."

His pronouncement nettled her. Was he telling her that because she was truly in danger or because Nathan had prompted him to do so? "For how long?"

"Let me make a couple calls."

While he took measurements and talked on the phone, Emma retreated to the small second bedroom where she'd set up her equipment. She could spare no time or energy debating whether or not she should stay in the loft. After Addison had left yesterday, Emma had gone through her inventory to get an idea of how far she would need to dip into her account to make enough jewelry for the show.

She pulled out her design pad and flipped through the sketches she had made over the last few months. Something tugged at her, an elusive notion of what the designs were missing. She turned to a blank page and let her pencil flow across the paper.

The contractor found her in the room a short time later. "I have someone who can come by tomorrow to take a look at your bathroom. His schedule's pretty full but he can probably get a crew here in ten days or so. Do you have someplace you can stay until the mold is removed?"

"That long?" She blew out a breath. "Do I really need to move out?"

"I definitely think it's a good idea."

Emma walked the contractor to the door and returned to her workroom. She didn't want to deal with packing up and moving. Especially not to Nathan's condo where prolonged exposure to his sex appeal would weaken her determination not to tumble into bed with him again.

She resumed flipping through her sketchpad, hoping to recapture her creative spark. Frustration filled her as focus eluded her. She couldn't stop thinking about Nathan's intoxicating kisses yesterday. Her skin tingled. Blood raced hot and frantic through her veins, pooling in the sweet spot between her thighs. She shifted on her stool, willing the impatient urges away.

She didn't have time to be distracted. With three weeks until the show, she would need to be focused on her jewelry every second. That meant no thinking about a certain handsome millionaire businessman who drove her crazy in every possible way.

Shaking her head, Emma told her traitorous pulse to settle down and picked up her pencil once more. Sometime later, her phone began to ring, waking her out of a creative fog. As the call rolled to voice mail, she sifted through all the new designs she'd come up with and smiled.

Her stomach growled, so she headed into the kitchen to heat up the leftovers of Nathan's soup for lunch. While she ate, Emma gazed around the outdated cabinets and appliances. She'd heard a great deal of criticism from everyone who'd seen the loft, but despite all the negative comments, Emma loved the space—imperfections and all—and the possibilities it represented.

She'd bought it a year ago, loving the high ceilings and the industrial feel of the exposed ductwork and brick walls. The front door opened into a large space she used as a combination living room and dining room. Shortly before she'd moved in, she'd had the hardwood floors refinished and they gleamed as they stretched across the inviting space. She'd furnished the living room with a comfortable gray couch and two blue armchairs the shade of Texas bluebonnets. The same blue broke up the expanse of white walls in the form of landscape photographs.

Her phone rang again as she washed her bowl and glass by hand. The dishwasher had died two months ago. Yet another thing that needed fixing.

She let this call go to voice mail as well. She guessed it was Nathan calling to badger her about moving in with him again. Well, that wasn't going to happen.

Returning to her workroom, she surveyed her equipment and the supplies scattered around the space. It would take her a day or more to get everything organized to move. She didn't have that much time to waste.

Nathan was just going to have to accept that she wasn't going to pack and she wasn't going to move. He wasn't her boss.

With a dismissive snort, she returned to her project and banished a tall, hunky millionaire from her mind.

"What do you mean she refuses to go anywhere?" Nathan barked into his cell phone. The mover he'd hired sputtered excuses as Nathan strode through Case Consolidated Holdings' parking garage toward his car. Two days ago his contractor had told her it was dangerous for her to remain in the loft, exposed to the mold.

Stubborn woman. He'd been all set to head home and find Emma all settled in, only to hear that she continued to defy him.

Nathan unlocked his car and tossed in his briefcase, breathing deeply to calm down. He was taking his frustrations out on the wrong person. "Why don't you guys grab dinner on me while I sort everything out?"

Ten minutes later he advanced down the hallway toward her loft. When Emma answered his impatient summons, she actually looked surprised to see him. Then, a mutinous expression settled over her beautiful face.

"What are you doing here?"

Despite her unfriendly question, his nerve endings sizzled and popped. She'd pulled her long, dark hair into a ponytail. Worn denim hugged her hips and a baggy sweater dipped off one golden shoulder, baring a purple bra strap.

He leaned his shoulder against the wall, realizing that he'd rather hear "no" from her than "yes" from any other woman.

"Nice to see you, too," he purred. Arguing with her was getting him nowhere. He needed to switch tactics. "Get changed. I'm taking you to dinner."

"I don't have—"

"Time. Yes, I know. But you have to eat, and I doubt there's anything edible in your refrigerator. Take a little break. You'll feel more up to working when you get back."

"And spend the whole meal being bullied by you into doing what you want me to do? No thanks."

"How about we only talk about the things you're interested in?" He offered her a neutral smile.

"No badgering?" she prompted. "No attempts at persuasion?"

He raised his right hand as if he was swearing in a court of law. "None."

"Oh, all right," she muttered ungraciously. "Give me a couple minutes to change."

While Emma retreated into her bedroom, Nathan called the movers and gave them new instructions.

For two days, he'd spent a good chunk of his time imagining the changes she would make in his life. His decision to marry her might have been born out of necessity, but lately he found himself thinking less about business and more about pleasure.

Unfortunately, standing in the way of those days and nights of unbridled passion was her stubbornness and this ridiculous wager with her father that she couldn't hope to win.

There was no way she could put the money back in her account by Valentine's Day, but that wouldn't stop her from trying. And he had his own deadline to worry about. He'd convinced his brothers to give him until the middle of February to secure the deal with Montgomery Oil. He couldn't do that without marrying Emma. The best way to do that was to make sure she had no way to win her wager. And the best way to do that would be to keep her too busy to work.

His groin stirred at the notion of all the things he would do to her once he moved her under his roof. She'd been without a decent bathroom for quite a while. Wait until she set eyes on the whirlpool tub in his master bathroom. It was made for long, romantic soaks. With candles burning, he'd even let her put bubble bath in the water. Hell, he'd do whatever it took to encourage her to join him.

He was still grinning ten minutes later when she crossed the living room toward him, her hips swaying in that natural motion that drove him crazy.

She'd donned a narrow, caramel-colored skirt with a wide ruffle that kissed her knees and a blouse of cream lace that revealed flirtatious hints of her creamy skin. Her brown hair had been twisted into a loose knot atop her head. She carried a brown velvet jacket that matched the color of her eyes.

"Where to?" she asked, fastening intricately woven earrings of gold wire studded with green freshwater pearls to her earlobes. They tapped against her neck, drawing Nathan's attention to the tender, sensitive skin.

"It's a surprise," he answered.

She didn't press him for details as he took her keys and

inserted them in the dead-bolt lock. She didn't utter a word until they were in his car, heading away from downtown. Then, she took hold of the conversational reins and steered them toward a safe topic.

"How do you like working with your brothers?"

"That question might take me all night to answer," he retorted.

"We don't have all night," she reminded him. "So you'd better get started now."

"We could have all night."

As her gaze played hide-and-seek with his from beneath her long bangs, he tightened his grip on the steering wheel to resist the urge to brush the sable locks away from her eyes. He had the crazy idea that if he looked deep enough, he would find that they wanted the same things, only she was too afraid to admit it.

"How long have you worked at Case Consolidated Holdings?" she asked, avoiding being pulled into flirting with him.

For the moment Nathan gave up trying to provoke her into a sexy repartee. He knew two ways to convince her that marriage between them made sense: to get to know her better and to get her back into bed. Since the latter was out of the question at the moment, he decided to focus on something that held equal appeal, making a connection.

"Six months."

"What did you do before that?"

So it was to be the third degree. Nathan split his attention between the road and the sexy lady sitting beside him. "I was in New York."

"That answers where you were, not what you were doing."

"I was making money in the stock market and attending auctions."

"Is that where you learned so much about art?"

"I had some good teachers. One woman I met loved the galleries and supported quite a few new artists. She had an eye for gifted young talent."

Emma hummed knowingly. "And were you one of the talented young men she had an eye for?"

"Are you asking if we were lovers?" he asked, amused by her perception of him as an innocent youth being corrupted by an older, more experienced woman. "No. She wasn't my type. I like curvy brunettes, remember?"

"And she wasn't either of those things?"

"No, Madeline had the look of a half-starved jungle cat. And she could be equally dangerous. Lucky for me she took a shine to my Texas accent and deep pockets. We were great friends. She had a ball trying to polish all my rough edges."

"I can't picture you in New York."

She squinted at him as if trying to put him in different clothes. He'd prefer if she'd just strip him out of the ones he currently had on. That pesky desire stirred again.

"I didn't blend in well," he agreed.

"Is that why you left?"

"No, I left because my father had a heart attack earlier this year and his doctor told him if he didn't slow down, the next one might kill him. He asked me to come work with Sebastian and Max. He thinks all three Case brothers belonged at the company our grandfather built." A thread of self-disgust ran through his explanation. "They certainly belong there. However, they're not convinced that I do."

"And why is that?"

He looked askance at her, wondering how much she knew about him. "Sebastian and Max are my half brothers."

"Cody said your father was having an affair with your mother and that you came to live with your father and half brothers after she died."

Just like that, his past was on the table, and his illegitimacy didn't seem to bother Emma one bit. "I was twelve when she died. Sebastian and Max weren't exactly thrilled to find out they had a half brother."

"I'm sure it was hard on all of you." There was understanding in her voice and comfort in the hand that covered his. "I'm sorry you lost your mom so young."

Something unraveled in his chest. Her sympathy exposed a place he'd walled up the day his mother died, a place he guarded against intruders. For a split second he wanted to share with her how much it had hurt to lose the one person in the world who'd loved him.

Instead, he shrugged.

"My brothers made my life hell. I moved out when I turned eighteen, kept moving after college."

"I'm surprised you came back after all these years."

"I wouldn't have if Dad hadn't called me."

Her eyes narrowed as she gazed his way. "I think there's more to it than that."

Did she see how much he wanted to best his brothers? To wipe Max's smirk right off his face and know he was responsible for the defeat in Sebastian's eyes?

"Maybe I want a chance to prove they've been wrong about me all these years. To make them admit I'm the one who should be running the family business. That's why this deal with your dad is so important."

Her hand fell away from his. Watching her knit her fingers in her lap, Nathan knew he shouldn't have resurrected the idea that his reasons for pursuing her were more practical than personal. But her compassion had touched a tender spot, and he'd flinched.

Nathan passed a semi and returned to the right lane. Time to change the subject. "How did you get into jewelry making?"

"I have a degree in sculpture from the University of Houston. I knew I wanted to make jewelry from the time I was six and I got one of those bead kits for Christmas. I drove everyone crazy with my necklaces and bracelets. I made one for my father. He even wore it once."

Nathan tried to imagine Silas Montgomery, the stiff, forceful businessman, wearing a necklace of bright-colored plastic beads around his neck. "So that's how you know so much about early Texas artists. I'm assuming your curriculum included a little art history."

"It did. But you've made me realize that I need to expand my knowledge base."

"I'd be happy to take you to an auction at Sotheby's. We could retrace my plunge into the dissolute world of art collecting."

"A trip to New York to gallery-hop." Her voice softened with longing. "That sounds like heaven."

Nathan glanced at her and wished he hadn't. The dreamy expression on her face reminded him of how she'd looked moments before her friend had interrupted them. His chest tightened. His groin stirred. And he heaved a sigh.

Tonight, whether she was ready for it or not, he was going to make something memorable happen.

Six

Emma watched Nathan navigate the Houston traffic and tried to harden her heart against the lost boy she'd glimpsed a moment earlier. An impossible task now that she understood a little bit more about what made him tick. He wasn't the unfeeling businessman who thought only of money and deals. But that didn't mean he wouldn't ruthlessly stomp all over her heart in pursuit of his agenda. Which meant, the more charming he became, the more she needed to be wary.

"Where are we headed?" she asked, her stomach seizing up with hunger pangs and anxiety.

He'd been a little too nonchalant about her continued determination not to move out of the loft. She knew he'd arrived tonight because she'd stonewalled the men sent to remove her things, but he hadn't mentioned it, and that aroused her suspicions.

"I thought we'd try Mark's American Cuisine."

Knowing their destination was a public place didn't settle her nerves the way it should have. She'd been convinced he was taking her to his condo to ply her with red wine and sex appeal until her resistance dissolved. To her immense shock, she was disappointed that he had no such nefarious plans.

"I haven't been there," she admitted. "But the food is supposed to be wonderful."

"I hadn't heard about the food," he said, casting a wry grin her way. "I was taking you there for the ambiance."

Mark's had been voted Houston's most romantic restaurant. "Is that so?" she quizzed, her tension unraveling beneath his flirtatious smile.

"That's so."

At the restaurant she waited while he came around the car and opened her door. As he pulled her to her feet, her heel caught in a hole. Unbalanced, she stumbled against his long frame. He caught her by the shoulders. Her heart stopped as the heat of his body enveloped her.

He hummed. "You know, we could grab some takeout and head back to my place."

Now, that was the Nathan she knew and...

"You were bringing me here for the ambiance," she reminded him, her eyes half closing as his warm breath stroked her cheek.

"My place has a great ambiance. Perfect for just the two of us."

And she wanted to go. So much. Despite the warnings from her rational side. Giving in now would signal Nathan that he'd won. He'd become even more relentless.

Her earrings tickled her neck as she shook her head. "Now that we're here, nothing could persuade me to leave without tasting Chef Mark's food."

"What about a chance to taste me?" The dare in his quicksilver-gray eyes touched her like a caress. She trembled.

What madness had led her to believe she could master her

attraction to Nathan? It throbbed in her body like a drumbeat, insistent, steady, increasing to a heady climax.

"You can be dessert," she whispered.

His eyes widened at her response. "After dinner we'll stop and buy some whipped cream."

Gulping, she grasped at something to defuse the sudden influx of sexual tension. Teasing him seemed to be the best way. "You don't think you're sweet enough for me?"

His grin blindsided her.

"Not by a long shot."

Emma gave him a shaky smile in return and lifted onto the balls of her feet to kiss him on the chin. "Then bring on the whipped cream."

"Dammit, woman," he muttered, guiding her inside the restaurant. "How the hell am I supposed to enjoy dinner when all I can think about is dessert?"

He sounded as disturbed as she felt. Emma's head spun at the notion that she had some power over him. He wasn't completely in control. Knowing that leveled the playing field a bit and relaxed her.

"You'll just have to manage," she said, squeezing his arm. "This is beautiful."

Located in a renovated church, the restaurant lived up to its reputation for romantic dining. The soaring cathedral ceiling, awash in golden light, arched over candlelit tables with white tablecloths and elegant place settings. A graceful staircase curved upward to what had once been the choir loft, now open to the tables below and edged with simple wrought-iron railing. The ceiling's line was echoed in the detailing above the doorways, drawing the eye upward.

The dining experience was everything she expected it to be. Won over by the candlelight, her charismatic dinner companion and way too much food, Emma set down her fork and spread her fingers over her stomach.

"That was delicious," she said, feeling sleepy despite

turning down the wine Nathan had ordered. Although the evening had taken on an enchanted glow, she needed to return to her loft and get back to work. Alcohol would have made that task impossible. "I can't recall the last time I ate so much."

"I have to admit, I do enjoy watching you eat. There's something so very sexy about it."

She made a face at him.

"Did you save room for dessert?" their waiter asked.

Emma welcomed his arrival because it kept her from having to answer Nathan. "I'm afraid I couldn't eat another bite."

Then she remembered her earlier dessert conversation with Nathan and her cheeks warmed. She glanced his way. A silver flame kindled in his eyes. Despite the large amount of food he'd consumed, there remained a hungry look about him. He appeared ready to devour her. A slow, steady heat crept through her, moving with determination to the parts of her most vulnerable to the persuasive power of desire.

"About dessert," she began, sounding unsteady and breathless.

The way his eyes slid over her made her quake. Traitorous longings weakened her resolve to go back to work tonight. Nathan Case, covered in whipped cream, was too much temptation for her to resist. And Emma had never been one to deny herself something she wanted. Hence, her current predicament.

She cleared her throat and tried again. "I really have a lot of work to do tonight. I should get back to my loft. There's so much to be done for the show. I'm starting with almost no inventory. The more pieces I make, the more I will have to sell and the better the show will go." She was babbling, but stopping the words from flowing off her tongue was nearly impossible, pierced as she was by those quicksilver eyes dancing with carnal promises.

"I understand," he said. "As long as you promise to give me a rain check on dessert."

With his hand warm on the small of her back, Emma let him guide her between the tables and out the door. "I'm not sure if a rain check is such a good idea."

As they waited for the valet to bring the car around, Nathan turned her toward him and cupped her upper arms in his hands. "Shh. Don't say something you'll regret."

Amusement fought with annoyance at his arrogance. She was trying not to *do* something she would regret.

Suddenly, Emma wondered why she was resisting the pull between them. Maybe she should just get him out of her system, and let him get her out of his. Then this business of her father's could dry up like a creek bed during a drought.

Once they were in Nathan's car, he turned left out of the parking lot instead of making the right that would take them back toward her loft. Emma got that funny feeling in her stomach again.

"Where are we going?"

"I thought we'd swing by my condo so I can return your earrings," he said as if this hadn't been his plan all along. "You said you wanted them back."

To claim otherwise would make him wonder why she was so skittish about the detour. Maybe he had no ulterior motives. Emma glanced at Nathan's profile. His lips had softened into a sensual curve. Excitement raced along her nerves as she recognized his expression. Oh, he definitely had ulterior motives.

Her breath shortened as anticipation seized her. Struggling to quell her body's thrumming need, she tore her attention from Nathan and watched the city slide by her window. By the time he drew up in front of his house, she was a tangled mess of sizzling hormones.

"Can't I just wait here while you get them?" she asked as he opened her car door. "I really have work to do."

He shook his head and held out his hand. With a gusty sigh, Emma let him pull her from the car. He slid his palm into the small of her back as they crossed the elegant lobby and ascended in the elevator. Her heart thumped hard enough to hurt as she recalled the last time she'd gone to his condo with him.

If his thoughts ran along the same lines, Emma couldn't tell from his bland expression. She half expected him to close his front door and pin her against it the way he had a month ago. Of course, last time, they'd both known why they'd come to his condo. The chemistry between them had been hot and inescapable. This time, Emma stepped into his foyer with a cooler head.

She didn't realize that she was holding her breath until they reached the condo's main living space. Letting the air flow out of her lungs, she stepped away from Nathan's tempting presence and scanned the room. A leather sectional occupied one end of the large open-concept floor plan; beyond that, a dining table was surrounded by ten chairs.

"What do you think?"

"About what?"

"My home." He smirked at her. "The last time you were here, we never made it out of the foyer."

Her cheeks burned as she recalled how he had taken her by storm. His urgency had thrilled her. Never in her life had a man wanted her with such intensity. Half closing her eyes, she relived the sensation of him sliding into her. The memory flushed her skin hot, arousing her.

She took in the view of downtown Houston visible through the floor-to-ceiling windows.

"It's very nice. But I'm not staying. I just came up to get my earrings."

He circled her like a tomcat on the prowl, his shoulder brushing across her back, his chest grazing her breasts as he stopped in front of her. Leaning forward, he whispered in her ear, "Are you sure that's the only reason?"

"Of course," she retorted, all the desire he aroused reducing her voice to a husky rasp. She had to get out of here. But her knees wobbled too much to let her escape.

"Because I was hoping I could get you to stay for a drink," he said, his hands sliding around her waist.

He nuzzled her neck, zeroing in on the spot that made her gasp. Her nipples tightened into hard beads of sensation. Her breasts felt heavy, ready for his possession. She swayed into his body, sighing as he flattened his palms against her butt, lifting her onto her toes, aligning her curves against his hard planes.

"I really shouldn't," she told him, her body liquefying as wave after wave of longing washed over her. "I've got work to do." She was beginning to sound like a broken record.

"Later," he growled against her lips before flicking his tongue against hers, stealing her breath and her sanity.

Sliding her hands up his chest, she buried her fingers in his hair and held on as he deepened the kiss, plundering her mouth, demanding that she respond without reluctance or hesitation. She surrendered to the hands that molded her body, the fierce seduction of his mouth stripping away her reservations about the lovemaking to come.

Lust ravaged her, destroying her last qualm. Her body belonged to him. He'd proved that the last time. And she trusted that he would be the perfect guide on this excursion into carnal delights.

"Tonight, we're going to do this slowly." He slipped his lips over her chin, her cheek, her eyes, her nose. "Last time you rushed me. That will not happen again."

Her head fell back as his teeth nibbled her earlobe. His ministrations ripped an airy giggle from her throat. "Not too slowly, or I might change my mind."

"I have no worries about that," he murmured, sounding

smug, the way a man with an armful of wanton woman would.

"Oh, for heaven's sake," she sighed, rubbing her pelvis against him in restless frustration as his palms kneaded her hips. Only with Nathan did she experience such riotous sensations. "I have so much pressure inside me, I'm going to burst."

She demonstrated the serious nature of her distress by moving against him in a manner that aroused her more than it eased her suffering. Nathan's mouth collided with hers as their hips began to rock together in a pantomime of what was to come.

"You have no idea what you do to me, Emma."

His words stoked the flames higher. Emma increased the abandoned gyrations of her body, too caught up in the heady turbulence to want a slow seduction. She knew he wanted their next time together to be in bed, but she was ready to throw him to the couch and straddle him.

Eager to see every gorgeous inch of him, she tugged his shirt free of his trousers, frantic to feel the warm silk of his skin. Nathan eased the pressure on her mouth long enough to aid her.

Together they dispensed with his buttons. With his shirt gone and her fingers against his skin, Emma purred with satisfaction. Urgency became awe as she skimmed the smoothness of his shoulders and the lean brawn beneath.

"You are beautiful." Hard muscles shifted beneath her exploring caress.

"I've never been called beautiful before."

"You are," Emma assured him, trailing her fingers across his chest and boldly tracing the path of rough hair to the place where it disappeared beneath his pants. "Now take everything off."

Nathan groaned as her provocative words and saucy tone impacted on the one area of his body he couldn't control. If he had been hard from the moment they'd stepped into the condo, he was ready to burst his seams after that comment.

She leaned forward and stroked her tongue against his collarbone, grazing his shoulder with her teeth.

"You first," he said. He couldn't trust his voice any more than he could count on controlling the rest of his body.

His desire for her ran fierce and resolute through his veins, but he bound it with relentless control. She deserved a slow, sensual ride. He wanted to bring her the same wild, unbridled pleasure her touch promised him.

"So, let's start with this." Emma stripped off her jacket and reached for the hem of her lace top, lifting it over her head, disturbing her careless topknot as she did so. She emerged from the cream material and gave her head a vigorous shake.

Nathan's breath caught. Long brown hair tumbled about her shoulders, framing a face of vulnerable beauty. He considered the wide-eyed darkness of her chocolate-hued eyes and the thoroughly plundered redness of her mouth.

Had he only kissed her? She looked positively drugged by passion.

"Now, that's more like it," he said an instant before her hands snaked out and caught his belt to tug him closer. He bent his head and answered her urgent call for a kiss.

Her lips clung to his when he lifted his head. She breathed in a rapid, unsteady manner that made him smile as he surveyed the wholly sensual look on her face, put there by his caresses.

Groaning low in her throat, the animalistic sound fanning his desire, she slid her palm downward. Before she could touch him, Nathan caught her wrist and pulled her hand away. "None of that right now. I promised you a night to remember," he growled, sweeping her off her feet and into his arms. "Not a quickie on the floor in my living room."

When he set her on her feet once more, his king-size mattress bumped the back of her knees.

"A quickie," she murmured, fumbling to unfasten the belt and the top button of his trousers. "Yes, make love to me now."

He tumbled her onto the bed. "If you insist."

"I insist." She arched, catlike, as he rolled her beneath him.

Nathan dipped his tongue in her ear and elicited a disturbed shudder, and then he leaned back to consider her smooth, pale skin and the provocative charm of her rose-tipped breasts, glimpsed through the lace of her bra.

"You are so soft," he sighed against her throat, trailing his tongue down her chest and across the delicate fabric of her bra.

She arched and offered her breasts. He felt her nipple harden after he raked his teeth across it. Her breath rasped in and out of her lungs, keeping time with the disturbed movements of her hands in his hair and across his shoulders.

"I've never felt anything like this before."

Her muted, feminine voice entered his system like the resonance of pure crystal, brightening his mood. "Good."

He rolled onto his back, taking her with him. With a hand on each thigh, he positioned her on top of him. He held her head and devoured her mouth, plunging his tongue deep to tangle with hers. As she gave him back all the passion he demanded, Nathan found his control slipping a little further from his grasp.

He'd intended to seduce her slowly, to ply her body with all the expertise at his disposal, but she moved against him frantically, her thighs tightening on his hips. Desire raked long talons across his senses. He was dangerously close to letting the urge to take her hard, deep and fast dictate his actions.

Without warning she broke off the kiss and sat up. She

rubbed her thumb across his lower lip. He nipped at the pad. Her lips curved in a satisfied smile as she stroked lower, sampling the shape of his chin, the sensitivity of his ears and the pulse throbbing in his throat.

"You have a very nice chest," she told him, drawing provocative circles in ever-tightening swirls around his pectoral muscles.

"I was thinking the same thing about you."

He lifted one hand to skim across her breasts just above the lace edging of the bra. Their pale roundness moved enticingly with each shuddering breath.

When he grazed her nipple through the satin fabric, she mimicked him. The sensation startled him. His erection prodded her through their clothes, insistent, relentless.

She shook her head, sending her long hair cascading around her face. Leaning down, she brushed the brown silkiness against his chest, tickling him, tantalizing him and hiding her expression.

"How does it feel when I touch you like this?" she asked, raking her nails over his nipples and down his abdomen.

"Incredible. How about when I touch you like this?" He swallowed her breasts in his hands and gently kneaded.

She threw back her head and arched her spine, putting her hands behind her and pushing into his caress. "Amazing."

Inspired by her husky, awed comment, he slowly rid them both of the rest of their clothes, taking the time to slide his hands and mouth over each new inch of her flesh he bared, until they were both naked and shaking uncontrollably. Emma's lashes veiled the expression in her eyes as Nathan drew the tip of one finger along the curve of her breast to her nipple. He watched her shiver as he slowly bent his head to capture the hard bud in his mouth.

"Oh, Nathan," she whispered his name as his mouth tugged at her breast.

"Are you cold?" he questioned, kissing his way down

her stomach to dip his tongue into her navel. Emma's gaze remained riveted on him as he lifted her thigh so that he could kiss the inside of her knee.

"No." Her voice broke as he opened his mouth and sucked on the sensitive flesh a little higher up. She rocked her hips, enticing him to touch where she ached.

"You're trembling."

"That's your fault."

"Let's see what I can do about it then."

His tone might have been affectionate and teasing, but his chest tightened with driving need. He eased his fingers along her thigh, aiming for the source of her pleasure. He caught and held her gaze while he brushed the brown curls at the juncture of her thighs. Her lashes fluttered, but she bravely watched. This open, visual lovemaking would drive him mad. Ah, but what a way to go.

The swirling pressure in his groin built into a knot of searing demand as Nathan slid his finger against her warmth, focusing her pleasure where he wanted it. Her eager reactions filled him with fierce satisfaction. He intended for her to feel the same wildness that was clawing him.

Her head moved restlessly against the pillow as he stroked her, pushing her toward the beckoning promise of fulfillment. She gripped the sheets, tension riding her curvaceous frame. The sounds of pleasure she made told him exactly how to increase the sensations roiling her.

"That's it, love," he crooned as she fragmented, her body rocked by a powerful orgasm. He held her while she gasped for breath, soothing her with long, sweeping caresses.

She tugged on his arm, urging him up beside her, and threaded her fingers through his hair. He kissed her nose and traced the line of her lower lip with his tongue, his body tight with need.

"Nathan?"

"Yes, Emma?"

"That was incredible." She parted her legs and rotated her hips until he was trapped in the sexy cradle between her thighs. "But I need more."

Her heat called to him, drove him mad with wanting. He kissed his way down her neck. "What's the rush? We have all night."

"You want to make me yours," she reminded him, nipping at his chin. Her breath hitched as he eased his lips over her skin. "Please do that."

He closed his eyes as her pleading eroded his willpower. "I want you fully satisfied before I do so. I don't think I've fulfilled my end of the bargain."

His voice shook with harsh urgency, but he couldn't control that any more than he could stop the trembling in his muscles as her fingers caressed his chest and moved lower. He wanted her so much he thought he might die from the ache.

"I won't be fully satisfied until you're inside me."

Nathan sucked in his breath as her fingers found his shaft and measured him in a series of provocative, fluid strokes.

No more words were needed. He eased forward. Her hips lifted to find the hardness of him and her hands cupped his buttocks to urge him into her. Trapped between her heat and the soft determination of her hands, he had no choice but to give her what she wanted.

Bracing his weight on his arms, he slipped inside her a little at a time. She groaned in pleasure as her body absorbed all of him. The sound almost pushed him over the edge, but he sucked in a deep, steadying breath and focused on her face.

"Tell me what you're thinking," he said, taking a long moment to savor the passion-drugged sleepiness in her heavy-lidded expression.

"I'm thinking…" she answered in a soft, cautious voice, digging her nails into his butt. Nathan's body jumped in response to her provocative caress. "That I've never been so turned on before."

"That's good."

He eased out of her as slowly as he had entered and watched her eyes round and darken until they were all pupil. She bit her lip. He clenched his teeth together to keep himself from slamming into her repeatedly and gaining the exquisite release his body craved. When he came, he wanted her with him.

The satisfying friction as he moved in and out of her blew huge, gaping holes in his willpower, but he started replaying multiplication tables in his head and held on.

She increased his tempo much sooner than he wanted. Her soft cries and the frantic movement of her hips destroyed the control he had fought so hard to maintain. The shattering of his heart began the moment he felt her release. Nathan gathered her into his arms and pounded his way to his own climax, enthralled by the way she kept pace with him. Together, they stormed into the brilliance of pleasure so acute he couldn't breathe.

As his name left her lips, as her fingers dug into his shoulders, as his chest tightened with the intensity of his emotions, he banded her to his body and shook in reaction, dazzled by their turbulent lovemaking.

In the aftermath of the fire, Nathan stroked a strand of hair away from her cheek and placed a gentle kiss on her lips, sensing that, at last, he'd found the woman who could curb his restless nature.

Seven

According to the digital clock on the nightstand, it was a quarter after five. Emma yawned. Falling asleep had been a mistake. Already she could feel herself falling under Nathan's spell. Spending the night and following that up with morning lovemaking would set a precedent Nathan would exploit to the fullest.

Although he hadn't mentioned marriage or even referred to an unofficial engagement between them last night, Emma knew his mind-set. He needed the deal with her father and would do whatever it took to persuade her to marry him, including seduce her limp and senseless over and over until she could refuse him nothing. But she had more immediate concerns.

Easing from beneath Nathan's arm proved difficult for several reasons.

Huge muscles were heavy.

His big naked body held as much temptation relaxed in sleep as it had aroused.

And he'd worn her out with the most incredible lovemaking she'd ever experienced.

As she swung her feet to the floor, Nathan stirred and reached toward her. She scooted off the bed and glanced over her shoulder, wondering if he'd awaken. He slumbered on, face half-buried in her pillow, his muscular torso sprawled across the space she'd so recently occupied. Ignoring the voice in her head encouraging her to wake him up for one last hurrah, Emma searched the dark room for her discarded clothes.

She nearly tripped over her skirt. Her bra lay three feet away. When had she kicked off her shoes? She paused to drape Nathan's pants across the foot of his bed. His shirt followed after she put the garment to her nose for a deep hit of the cologne he wore. The same scent emanated from her skin. She smiled, wondering if the hands he'd smoothed over every inch of her skin smelled like Donna Karan's Cashmere Mist.

A groan gathered in her throat. Why hadn't she honored the promises to herself and stayed out of Nathan's bed? Who was she kidding—the instant his mouth settled on hers, stealing her breath, demanding her surrender, she'd been putty in his hands. He'd wrung impassioned moans from her throat, sexy encouragement from her lips and uncontrolled writhing from her body. Her cheeks burned hot as she thought about all the things she had let him do.

She stared at the bed, eyeing the tangled sheets that bared his back and most of one butt cheek. Shockingly, the space between her thighs tingled. She bit down on her tender, well-kissed lips, fighting temptation. How could she possibly be ready for more?

Quit stalling. Get yourself dressed and get out.

The urge to pause for one last look at the slumbering man fought with her practical side. Hadn't she already over-indulged? Emma slipped on her lingerie and skirt, zipping it on the short walk into his living room, and dangled her shoes by the straps as she made her way to the door.

As each mile of the taxi ride home took her farther away from Nathan, her body came down off a sensual high. She felt the first twinge of a withdrawal headache as she put her key in the lock. By the time she swung the door open, her nerves were showing distinct signs of exposed edges. She felt strung out and weary beyond words.

Flipping on the lights, she stared at the empty room. Adrenaline surged, banishing any fatigue. What the hell had happened to her stuff?

She advanced into her loft and stopped where her couch should have been. Her heart jumped in her chest. Next, she pushed open the door to her workroom and stared at the bare space. No equipment. No supplies and finished pieces. Half-dazed, she crossed the hall to check out her bedroom. Furniture. Clothes. Everything she owned. Gone.

Emma closed her eyes. Her fingers tightened into fists.

Nathan.

He'd lured her out for a romantic dinner with assurances that he wouldn't persuade or bully her to move out of the loft. He'd plied her with flirtatious conversation until she'd fallen back into bed with him. Emma growled. All the while his movers had been busy clearing out her things. He must have had a good laugh at her expense tonight. What an idiot she was.

Thank goodness it was too early to call Addison. Emma wanted nothing more than to run to her best friend, borrow a pair of pajamas and curl up on her couch to whine about Nathan. Three months ago she would have done just that.

Her father's belief that she lacked drive wasn't a notion he'd pulled out of thin air. As a pampered and spoiled heiress, Emma was never expected to accomplish anything. As a result, she'd never taken charge of her life, just drifted through it.

But her expectations for herself had changed. And if she

intended to produce $35,000 worth of jewelry, she would have to go to Nathan and demand her equipment back.

She dug her car keys out of her purse and marched out the door. At half past five o'clock in the morning, few cars were on the road as she sped through town on her way back to Nathan's condo. She didn't bother to call him again, not wanting him to know she was coming. By the time she pulled into his parking lot, she'd worked herself into a fine fury.

Standing outside his door, she listened to her pounding heart and some of the urgency left her. She wasn't good at confrontation. Probably because she'd spent so much of her childhood surrounded by it. Her parents fought all the time. Fire from her mother. Ice from her father.

Nathan answered the door almost before she lifted her finger from his doorbell. Dressed in pajama bottoms, his muscular chest looming bare and magnificent before her eyes, he leaned his forearm against the doorframe and looked her up and down. "Well, hello. Did you run out for coffee and doughnuts?"

That he continued to play games with her, after taking her to dinner under false pretenses and then making love to her as if she was the most important woman on earth, revived her anger.

"Where's my stuff?"

He stepped back and gestured her inside. "Some of it's in storage. Some of it's here."

"I told you I didn't want to move." She crossed the threshold and pulverized his grin with a hard look. "Not in here with you. Not anywhere."

"Despite everybody telling you that staying in your place was a health hazard?" He shook his head.

She set her hands on her hips. "So you decided to steal all my stuff?"

"I didn't steal it." His measured tones infuriated her as

he tugged her deeper into the condo. "I moved it so the contractors I hired could get to work."

"You hired contractors?" she demanded, annoyed at how control over her life was slipping from her grasp. "It's my loft. I should be the one doing the hiring." She narrowed her eyes at his easy shrug and trailed after him as he headed into the kitchen. The scent of brewing coffee made her nose twitch with interest despite herself. "And I don't understand why everything is gone. Surely they don't need all my furniture removed to clean up a mold problem."

Nathan poured two cups of coffee and handed her one. "After leaving your loft yesterday, I realized that you can't sell it the way it is now."

"Sell it?" Emma wondered if she'd just heard him properly. "Why would I want to do that?"

"Because after we're married we'll live here."

The words *after we're married* reverberated through her head. He was taking a lot for granted. "I thought you understood that I'm not going to marry you because of some business deal."

"But you are going to marry me."

The man was insufferable.

"No, I'm not," she fumed. "And I'm not moving in with you, either."

He sipped coffee and watched her over the rim of the cup.

Emma stared back at him, matching his silence while her thoughts churned. How was she supposed to get all her pieces finished in time for the show? Then, it occurred to her that this had been his plan all along. If he stopped her from working, she wouldn't make enough to replace the money in her account and she'd be forced to marry him. Her heart skipped a beat. Was he that diabolical?

"Where's the equipment and supplies from my workroom?"

"In storage. Your clothes are in my guestroom."

Hadn't he heard a word she said? "I'll stay with Addison until the mold is cleaned up, then I'm moving back into the loft. Call your contractors and cancel them. I'm not going to do any remodeling on the loft because I'm not going to sell it." Her jaw hurt from clenching her teeth, but she managed to add, "I'll have someone in here either this afternoon or tomorrow to move my things out."

"And where do you plan to work? You'd better not go back to the loft."

"I'll find studio space I can rent."

"You can work here."

His offer was grudging at best. He didn't want her working at all. And Emma couldn't imagine getting anything done with his presence distracting her.

"You don't need to worry about me," she said, and wished her words would convince him.

"How can I help it?"

"Easy. Just remind yourself that I'm not your responsibility."

His dark eyebrows arched. "Not yet."

"Not ever."

"We'll see."

Nathan realized that he'd been staring at the set of financials for half an hour without making any sense of the numbers. In fact, he'd been distracted all morning. After five days of searching, Emma had been unable to find space to work. Desperate and running short on time, she'd ungraciously reconsidered her refusal of his spare bedroom as her studio, but spent her nights at her friend's house.

Despite knowing that he was her last option, he'd been pleased that Emma had stayed within his grasp, even if she'd wrung a promise from him not to sabotage her jewelry or interfere with her workspace.

This meant the only way to keep her from working would be to distract her with kisses and lovemaking, but like the shoemaker's elves, she was both industrious and elusive. In the four days since she'd been working in his condo, he had yet to catch sight of her.

Every night when he arrived home, he went straight to the spare room where her equipment was set up and noticed new sketches pinned to the walls and glittering works in progress scattered across her worktable.

And the more jewelry she finished, the more likely it was that she would make good on her threat to sell enough at the show to meet her goal. He needed to slow her down. An impossible task with all the long hours he was working at rehashing the numbers for the venture with Montgomery Oil.

Maybe he should take work home. Lord knew he could use a break from the office. His brothers' negative attitudes were getting on his nerves more than ever. For the last week, he'd been as surly as a bear awakened in the middle of winter.

He checked his watch. He could head home for lunch and surprise her with a little afternoon delight. Decision made, he grabbed his keys and the tube containing the architect's plans for her loft that he'd commissioned. Anticipation kicked him hard as he headed for the door. He dodged the implication that not seeing Emma was what accounted for his foul mood, but it dogged his heels in a relentless bid for attention.

He was moving briskly down the hall when Sebastian called after him. "Nathan, got a minute?"

Hissing in exasperation, Nathan turned and spied his older brother standing just outside his office. Sebastian must have seen him going by. "Sure," he said, retracing his steps. "What's up?"

"Max and I are heading out to meet with Lucas for a couple days." Sebastian gestured Nathan into his room. "I wondered if you had any input for us before we go."

Nathan noticed that he hadn't been included in the meeting. Resentment burned. They'd regret cutting him out of the decision-making process. He'd make sure of it. "I don't see the point. You won't like what I have to say."

Sebastian's mouth tightened at Nathan's sarcasm, but he wasn't as reactive as Max. "Maybe you should come along and say it in person."

Sebastian's offer surprised Nathan. Obviously, he and Max were still determined to persuade Lucas to sell his company, but it also appeared that they were willing to listen to Nathan's analysis of the business.

Or at least Sebastian was. Max hadn't voiced his opinion. But if Nathan could get one Case brother on his side, chances were the other one would come around in time. Divide and conquer.

Or was it possible that they were interested in finding some middle ground and starting a dialogue?

"When are you thinking of going?" Nathan asked, curious as to what his brothers were up to.

"We thought we'd go this week," Sebastian said.

He really should stick around Houston and prevent Emma from having uninterrupted access to her equipment and supplies at his condo.

"Set up the meeting," Nathan said. "Let's see what Lucas has to say."

"Earth to Emma."

Distantly she heard her name and blinked to redirect her focus from the necklace on the worktable. Nathan lounged in the doorway, his shoulder propped against the frame. Dressed in a navy suit, pale blue shirt and red tie, he looked every inch the powerful executive in his prime. Emma's traitorous pulse lunged like a racehorse from the starting gate.

She'd been very careful to avoid him, keeping the hours she spent at the condo short to leave for Addison's before he arrived home. At first she hadn't wanted to run into him because she was still furious over the way he'd tricked her into moving out of her loft. Then, as her anger faded and the night she'd spent in his arms played repeatedly in her mind like a steamy foreign film, she'd steered clear of him out of a desire for sheer self-preservation.

She didn't trust herself to be alone in the condo with him and not succumb to his sizzling kisses again. Just the thought of him and her and an empty condo got her hot and bothered. He needed to believe that she wasn't going to fall for his winning charms and let him boss her around anymore.

Sifting through a pile of sapphires, she did her best to ignore the throb of awareness pulsing through her. If only he'd stop eyeing her as if she was a juicy apple he was dying to sink his teeth into. She almost groaned at her body's sharp reaction to the notion of his mouth on any part of her.

With the back of her hand, she brushed her bangs off her face. "How long have you been standing there?"

"A couple of minutes. You certainly seem preoccupied by what you were doing." He gestured with the long tube he carried.

"I have a lot to do and only ten days to get it done." She held up a half-finished necklace for his inspection, pleased by how well her design looked in gold. The light clipped to the side of her worktable made the diamonds sparkle. "But I'm doing some of my best work ever."

He cocked his head as he surveyed the necklace. "I'm glad to hear that."

Her insides twisted into an uncomfortable knot. To her dismay, she realized that she'd expected his eyes to light up with pride at her accomplishments. She wanted him to appreciate her craft and to understand how important this show was to her, not just because she needed to restore the money to her account, but also because it would prove that she could take care of herself by doing something she was great at.

What an idiot she was. Bad enough that he whipped her into a sexual frenzy with his lazy smiles. She'd really be setting herself up for heartache if his opinion of her started to matter.

Nathan tapped a roll of blueprints out of the tube he was holding and spread them across her worktable, using pliers, the box that held her loose stones, and the necklace she'd shown him to weigh down the corners.

"I brought you some sketches for the remodel on your loft."

She shook her head. Exhaustion dragged at her shoulders. "I don't have the money or the time to think about remodeling my loft right now."

"Let me do it."

"No." Emma bristled. He wanted to fix up her place to sell it. "Why won't you listen to me?"

Instead of reacting negatively to her sharp tone, Nathan left the sketches and circled her worktable. He'd come within reach before she caught the intent in his eye. Back against the wall, surrounded by equipment, she had no place to flee. She held up her tweezers.

Ignoring her defensive stance, he spun her around on her stool. His hands settled on her shoulders, thumbs rolling deep pressure into her muscles. Rather than feeling sexual, his touch pleasured her on a whole different level. She groaned her appreciation and let her head drop forward.

"You should take some time off," he told her, massaging his strong fingers down either side of her spine. "You're working too hard."

"I have to get ready for the show."

"You'll concentrate better if you're not so tired."

Did he know she wasn't sleeping? Crashing on Addison's couch wasn't ideal. Between staying up late to sketch new designs and her best friend's early-rising brood, she was lucky to snag four hours of shut-eye. The first few nights it hadn't been bad, but now, in the second week, she was feeling the effects of weariness. She'd messed up an important piece yesterday afternoon for that very reason, but she couldn't stop, much less slow down.

"I'll sleep when the show's over," she said, pulling away from his invigorating massage before he convinced her to take a break. His hands on her back made her long for him to apply that healing touch to other parts of her body, parts that were achy for reasons having nothing to do with jewelry-making. She fussed with the gems on her worktable. "Until then, I intend to work until I drop."

"Take five minutes and look at what my architect came up with."

Exhausted and awash with conflicting desires, she gave him a taste of her frustration. "What part of 'I'm not going to sell my condo' aren't you getting?" she muttered crossly. "Did it ever occur to you that I don't like being told what to do? You bullied me into moving out of my loft and now you tell me that you're going to remodel it so I can sell it because we're getting married. You've never once thought about what's best for me." Emma's chest heaved as she drew breath for her next onslaught of temper. "Go away, Nathan, and take your plans with you."

She indicated the ones he'd spread over the table, but really meant all his plans—the ones for her loft, the ones for her future and, most important, the ones for her heart. She moved the weights that held the floor plans flat and they curled up on themselves.

Emma returned to sorting sapphires, her hands shaking hard enough that she could barely pick up the pink gem she intended to place into the gold setting. Although Nathan was a difficult man to ignore, she put her heart and soul into it. He stood beside her for a long moment, impatience rolling off him, before he dropped a perfunctory kiss on the top of her head and walked out of the room.

An insistent ringing disturbed Nathan's grim thoughts. The meeting with Lucas Smythe had gone worse than he'd expected. The guy was definitely considering selling his company and offering Case Consolidated Holdings first crack at it. Sebastian and Max were full of smug delight and Nathan was fighting hard to stop them from shutting down his venture with Montgomery Oil. With three weeks to go until Valentine's Day, the only thing keeping his deal with Silas alive was the fact that Smythe was not one hundred percent ready to let go of the business his family had owned for the last hundred years.

Glancing at his cell phone's display, he took the call. "Hey, Dad."

Brandon Case's rich chuckle filled Nathan's ear. "Don't you sound cheerful. Your brothers giving you trouble?"

Nathan gestured to the bartender to bring him another whiskey and stared at the hockey game on the television behind the bar. "You know they are."

"How's the deal going with Montgomery?"

"We're talking a couple times a week. He's got his people confirming our financial forecast. Cody's looking into possible locations for the production facility."

"Sounds promising."

"Yeah." Nathan knew his dad couldn't possibly miss the lack of enthusiasm in his voice. He was under the gun from two quarters. His brothers were awfully enamored of Smythe's company. How long before they convinced the guy to sell? Nathan had little trouble imagining a scenario in which he convinced Emma to marry him, and then couldn't do the deal with her father because his brothers bought Smythe Industries. "But it all might be a big waste of time."

"Let me guess—Lucas Smythe's company?"

A cheer went up behind Nathan. Someone must have scored.

"It balances our product mix and provides Case Consolidated Holdings with conservative but steady growth," he muttered.

"I was right to convince you to come home. I love those boys, but neither one has any instincts when it comes to taking risk. Too much education."

Nathan rolled his head from side to side in an attempt to loosen the knots in his shoulders. "I don't think having advanced degrees in business makes Max and Sebastian risk-adverse."

"It's because they take after their mother," Brandon said. "Whereas you take after me and your mother. Never met anyone as strong and brave as Marissa."

It wasn't the first time Nathan had heard his father's tone grow wistful when he spoke about Marissa Connor, but it was the first time Nathan asked a particular question. "Did you love her?"

He had no idea what had prompted him to delve into the relationship between his parents after avoiding the topic for so many years. Maybe he'd been thinking too much about Emma this trip and pondering how to overcome her determination to marry for love. He'd called her each day he'd been gone, getting her voice mail and leaving messages both times. She'd returned his calls, but he'd been in meetings and she hadn't left a voice mail. He craved the sound of her voice right now. It bugged him just how much he wanted to talk to her.

"Love her?" Brandon sounded surprised. "I adored her."

Was that true? Or was it a man's fond remembrance of the woman he'd lost before he could grow tired of her?

"I only wished I'd met her before Susan and I got married," Brandon continued. "I would have saved everyone a lot of heartache if I'd held out for the girl of my dreams instead of deciding it was time to settle down."

His father's words were like a left jab that came out of nowhere. His father had settled for marriage without love and lived to regret it. Nathan lurched back from the uncertainty that had appeared before him like a sinkhole. "But you didn't leave Susan."

Brandon sighed. "I wanted to, but Marissa wouldn't let me. She said I had a family who needed me."

Unexpected pain blossomed in Nathan's chest. What about him and his mom? They'd needed Brandon, too. "You're lying," he growled. "She loved you. She'd smile and hum for days after you visited. Why would she tell you to stay married?"

"Because she was stronger than me. Than Susan. Than your brothers. You both were." Brandon's voice grew melancholy. "They needed me. You didn't. Not really. Together the two of you could take on the world. It's why I wanted you to work with your brothers. They need your strength. Your confidence. The three of you will do great things with the business."

"Maybe, but we have to learn to work together first," Nathan muttered bitterly.

"Do you want me to talk to them?" his dad asked, his voice gaining an edge. "They need to understand you're an equal partner."

Nathan knew his father was feeling restless since retiring. Brandon liked keeping tabs on the business and voicing his opinions. He didn't understand how much that irritated his eldest son.

"Thanks, Dad, but this is something I need to handle."

After hanging up, Nathan sipped his drink and let his thoughts drift toward Emma as they'd been doing all too often lately. Never before had he struggled so hard to keep his attention on business.

From the moment he'd boarded the plane in Houston, it had occurred to him that he was worried about leaving her to her own devices. Her inability to understand the limitations of her energy and strength irritated him. In the last glimpse he'd had of her before leaving on this trip, he'd seen that Emma was driving herself toward exhaustion.

Until he'd surprised her over lunch, he'd assumed that the only work she'd been doing had been at his condo, but seeing how pale she'd become since he'd moved her out of her loft, he'd gotten her to admit that she spent her nights crafting her designs.

Things were going to change when he got back. He was going to convince her to move in so he could keep an eye on her and make her slow down. It was past time she started accepting that her future was with him. Once they were married, she wouldn't need to make jewelry or worry about money. He would take care of her the way she deserved to be cared for.

Eight

"You have to eat something," Nathan said, standing bare-chested before her worktable, his dark hair wet from the shower. Worn denim rode low on his hips, and he'd brought the scent of lavender into the spare room.

He'd returned home from his business trip an hour ago, more grim than she'd ever seen him, and commenced badgering her to take a break as soon as his overcoat hit the hall closet.

Avoiding Nathan's gaze, Emma eyed the plate he held. Although the fat strawberries tempted her, her stomach shifted uncertainly. She hadn't been interested in food lately. She blamed it on anxiety. Progress was much slower than she'd anticipated, due to the intricate nature of her newest designs. Of course, the finished product made the extra hours worthwhile, but she was overwhelmed with the amount of work still to be done.

"I ate before you came home." Fatigue threatened to tip

her off the stool. She'd been perched on it so long her behind had gone numb.

"What time?" he demanded.

"What time is it now?"

Nathan glowered at her. "Seven o'clock."

That meant she'd been sitting at her worktable for twelve hours straight with only bathroom breaks and a quick snack sometime around one. For the last three days, she'd been practically living in this room, taking advantage of his absence to execute one piece of jewelry after another. Never in her life had she put so much effort into anything. It was as exhilarating as it was exhausting.

She'd jump for joy if she could summon the energy.

"A couple hours ago."

"You are many things, Emma Montgomery, but a skillful liar you are not."

"I'll eat in a minute." In truth, she was afraid to stop working. Afraid, because she was so exhausted, that she might never start again. The long hours were taking their toll on her mind as well as her body, but she had a significant inventory of jewelry to show for all her effort. Yet, so much remained unfinished and with the clock ticking down, her nerves were stretched as thin as onionskin.

"You keep saying that and yet you don't." Radiating frustration, he arched his eyebrows at her. Crossing his arms over his chest made his biceps bulge. "I'm not leaving here until I see you eat every bite of that sandwich."

"Which I'll do as soon as I finish this ring." Her hands trembled as she struggled to fix a tiny diamond into place on the platinum band she was working on. She hissed a curse. "I promise."

Tears gathered in her eyes. If the stupid diamond didn't settle into the cradle she'd crafted for it, she was going to scream.

The ring blurred. She blinked away the weariness eating

into muscle and bone. Just a couple more hours, and she could knock off for the night. A couple more hours and she could stumble back to Addison's couch.

All too aware of Nathan's keen watchfulness, she clenched her teeth against a yawn. The struggle was brief, and in the end, she lost.

"Enough. You're dead on your feet." He circled the worktable, handed her the plate and plucked her off the stool as easily as if she'd been a child.

"Put me down."

Her stomach growled while she glared at him. "I don't have time for this. I need to work."

"You need to eat and rest." He swept her out of the room and strode down the hall, passing the guestroom he'd repeatedly offered.

Her heart bounced fretfully in her chest as he passed the living room and kept going. "Where are you taking me?"

"Bed."

"Not your bed."

His answer was a slow smile.

She made her displeasure known by spouting objections and shoving the heel of her palm against his steely shoulder, but despite her resistance, desire awakened and banished her earlier tiredness. How could she continue to want him with such intensity when he acted like such a domineering oaf? Yet, even as she fought for independence, the heat of his skin penetrated her annoyance and a sensual longing defused her protests.

By the time he lowered her to the bed, she'd relaxed her fists, sent her palms coasting along the silken skin of his upper back and let her fingers tangle in his dark hair.

Catching the change in her mood, he joined her on the mattress, and reclined on his side. She set the plate between them.

He picked up a strawberry and offered it to her. "Please eat."

Emma pushed herself up on her elbow and opened her mouth. He set the fruit between her lips, approval and lust glowing in his eyes as her teeth sank into the ruby flesh. Luscious and sweet, it exploded on her tongue like a sensual bomb, awakening her senses. She licked juice off her lips as he picked up another strawberry. Long before she finished the last one, she had a thundering need to get her hands on the erection straining against Nathan's zipper.

Putting the uneaten sandwich on the nightstand, she brushed her fingers down the front of his jeans, watching his pupils dilate and his nostrils flare. Wicked delight rippled through her as she drew her nails upward along the same path. His hips shifted as she plucked at the button that held his jeans closed. Thrilled by his harsh breathing, she found the tab of his zipper and began to slide it down, one millimeter at a time.

"Emma." Her name erupted out of him like a plea.

"Yes, Nathan?"

Pushing her hands away, he unzipped and stripped off his jeans. In turn, she shimmied out of her shirt, sweatpants and underwear, flinging them aside in her impatience. In less than a minute they knelt on the mattress facing each other, naked, inches apart, lungs burning with the rush of air that flowed in and out.

Emma was the first to move. She reached down and took Nathan's hard length, sliding her hand up, then down. A roar rumbled in his chest. His shaft pulsed in response to her caress. Satisfaction blazed as he threw back his head and bared his teeth. Raw need poured from his throat, arousing her still further.

Longing to give him the same sort of pleasure he'd given her, she lowered her head. Before she could put her mouth on him and taste the silken texture of his erection or run her tongue around the head and up the sensitive vein on the underside, Nathan tumbled her onto the mattress.

Startled, Emma scraped the hair away from her face and searched his expression. Nathan knit their fingers together and rested their joined hands on the pillow beside her head. His stillness left her awash in uncertainty. Need pulsed through her. Days apart made her frantic for his long, deep kisses. Hungry for the possessive caress of his hands against her hot skin. She craved their joining as she had craved nothing ever before. Didn't he want that, too?

Something in Nathan's half-lidded gaze held her transfixed.

Emotion.

He dropped his lips to hers and made slow work of exploring her mouth. Lost in the stroke of his tongue, the sweet seduction of his breath against her neck, his teeth on her earlobe, she realized that it wasn't all about physical desire for him. He cared for her. Maybe not to the point of love, but this was neither casual nor forgettable for him. She'd tasted the truth in his kisses and the way he made sure she was completely satisfied before he took his own pleasure.

A knot formed in her chest. Pretending this was just sex between them was going to be a lot harder with what she'd just realized. And her heart was more at risk than ever. Because hope had been awakened. Hope that caring could become more. Could become love. Anything less would shred her heart.

Shoving away her worries, she concentrated on the heat building in her loins as his tongue swirled around her breast in languid circles. A gasp tore from her throat as his mouth settled over her hard nipple and suckled her. Pleasure shot straight to her core. His hand followed, stroking down her body, sweeping away her last coherent thought. He explored her with delicate care, finding a host of sensitive spots that inflamed her yearning for him to touch where she burned.

Nathan had always been a considerate lover, but today she

was too impatient, her desire too fiery, spiraling out of control. She wanted him to take her hard and fast.

"I need you." Emma's fingers bit into his shoulders. His weight pinned her to the mattress, but she could wiggle her hips, make him notice her hunger. "Inside me," she gasped as his fingers slid between their bodies and found her heat. "Now."

He obliged by shifting between her parted thighs, his knees against hers, opening her for his possession. Murmuring words of encouragement and appreciation against her hot skin, he braced his hands above her shoulders and rocked his hips forward, penetrating her with a quick, deep thrust. She arched her back and gripped his wrists as her world exploded in a dazzling shower of sensation. She opened her soul to the shattering wonder of their coming together and groaned in pleasure as her body expanded to accommodate his size.

When he was completely encased in her, he stilled, and dropped his cheek against hers. "Woman, you feel marvelous. Are you okay?"

With his weight pinning her to the mattress, their bodies fitted together as nature designed, she knew she'd never been better.

"Perfect." She breathed the word reverently and rocked her hips, taking him even more deeply inside until he rested against her womb. She felt a flutter of delight. The first promise of her climax to come.

He slid one hand beneath her, cupping her derriere in his palm as he began that incredible slide in and out of her body. Pressure built faster than she thought possible and lifted her high into the sky where she fractured and rained back to earth in a thousand pinpoints of light. She returned to her body, drawn back by Nathan's deep kisses.

"Next time we'll go together," he promised, resuming the long, slow thrusts that had pushed her over the edge the first time.

"I promise to try to be more patient," she panted, soothing his cheeks with her fingers. "It will help if you don't make me wait so long next time."

"Make *you* wait?" he growled, moving powerfully against her, driving deep into her core with spectacular results. "You've been avoiding me—" A groan escaped his lips as she tightened her internal muscles and felt him shudder in response.

It was so easy to please him. Everywhere she touched invoked a reaction. He seized her lips in a passionate kiss as their lovemaking became more and more frenzied. Then, a guttural roar proclaimed his own release as he surged into her one last time, before collapsing onto her.

With her arms wrapped around his shoulders, her legs around his hips, Emma savored the peaceful aftermath of their lovemaking, knowing the cease-fire wouldn't last. Soon he would slip out of her body and move away from her embrace, shattering the fragile intimacy created by the compelling attraction that exploded between them in bed.

Too soon, she would return to work and he would renew his efforts to distract her, but for now, she surrendered to the moment, feeling lazy and oh so very satisfied.

"Now, can we talk about how *I* made *you* wait," he murmured, kissing his way down her neck.

Despite being exhausted from the long hours she'd spent hunched over her worktable, Nathan's touch aroused her all over again. She'd spent so much time imagining the things she wanted to do in this bed. She had a dozen fantasies to live out.

"I'm not feeling much like talking," she said, rolling him onto his back and straddling him. Her breath hitched as he reached up and gently weighed her breasts in his hands.

"In other words, just enjoy this?"

She bent forward, her lips hovering just above his, and smiled. "Exactly."

* * *

Now this was more to his liking.

Nathan listened to the deep, steady breathing and inhaled the warm scent rising off the skin of the soft, naked woman sleeping in his arms. He took a long moment to savor the press of her full breasts against his chest and the tangle of their legs beneath the covers. Then, he opened his eyes and feasted on her passion-bruised mouth and long lashes. In the predawn light, with her mussed hair and naked shoulders rising out of the sheets, she appeared well-loved. His lips curved in a satisfied smirk.

When he'd first awakened, any thought of moving had been immediately rejected. The need for activity that drove him relentlessly had been tempered by the previous night's lovemaking. He wanted nothing more than to enjoy having Emma stretched out beside him. Parts of him, however, proved to have an abundance of energy. Blood surged into his groin, signaling a lust he'd thought well-sated.

Nathan slid his hand up her thigh and across her backside. He spread his fingers over the curve, applying pressure to ease her against his hard-on. Her lashes flickered, telling him she was awake. He nuzzled her temple.

"I have to go," she murmured, her muscles tensing as she braced to move.

He tightened his grip. If he let her escape, his contentment would go with her. What was happening to him that he could think of nothing better than spending the entire day in bed with her, just reading the paper or enjoying the feel of her body against his?

"Just stay a little longer."

"I've stayed too long already," she retorted, squirming against his grip, arousing him still more with her wriggling. "I've got work to do."

"Forget about the show. You'll never make your father's deadline."

"I'll make it." She glared at him and wedged her hands between their bodies to push him away. "I will make it."

"Why don't you just give up and marry me? You know I'll take care of you the way you were meant to be taken care of."

"I don't want to be taken care of."

Says the girl who wants a fairy-tale marriage, Nathan thought. If she'd give him half a chance, he could change her mind on that score, show her how thoroughly he could spoil her.

"Why are you fighting this so hard? We're great together. Last night was amazing."

Nathan rolled her beneath him, pinning her wrists above her head. Her muscles melted, body yielding. But her lips thinned in mutiny, and a resentful tempest darkened her eyes.

"Last night was about sex. That's not what I'm looking for in a marriage."

"It had better be or your husband will wander," he teased, nuzzling her neck, enjoying her skin.

"What I mean is sex isn't all I'm looking for in a marriage. I need love, too."

"Love doesn't last."

"Sometimes it does."

Feeling the tension in the slim body beneath his, Nathan released her wrists and shifted his weight off her. She slid out of bed.

His body ached as he watched her walk toward her discarded clothes. Was there anything sexier than a woman's back, he wondered, linking his fingers behind his head. The sheet slid to his waist, stopped from going farther by his morning erection. A cold shower would take care of that. In the meantime, he savored the dimples at the small of her back on either side of her spine, the sexy swoop of her narrow waist, and the flare of her heart-shaped derriere. She bent to retrieve her underwear, and he sighed as the action shoved her luscious tush into the air.

Keeping her back to him, she stepped into her pale pink panties. Watching her slide the scrap of lace into place was almost as sexy as watching her remove it. Everything about her turned him on. When she was done hooking her bra, she pivoted to face him.

"The man I marry will want me because of who I am, not because of who my father is."

Nathan leaned forward, running his eyes roaming over her half-naked form, filling the room with his desire for her. "I do want you."

"But you don't love me."

Could you?

The question peeked at him from beneath her long lashes. In her expression, he saw the barest hope that he might someday change his mind about love.

Cody's words came back to him. She wanted a fairy tale. A happily-ever-after. Is that what his mother had hoped for? His father's wife? His brother, Sebastian, whose marriage had disintegrated after two short years? Probably. Instead, they'd gotten heartbreak.

Her lips curved downward as the silence between them stretched out. He hated seeing her unhappy, but it wasn't fair to lead her on.

Finally, she got fed up with his lack of an answer. "I didn't think so," she muttered, scooping her shirt off the floor.

As much as he didn't like to be the source of her pain, she deserved his honesty. She needed to understand that she'd have his respect, his fidelity, his affection, just not his love.

And in the end, both of them would be happier for it.

"Love isn't what makes a marriage last," he said. "Or there wouldn't be half as many divorces. You need mutual respect and shared goals."

"I agree that marriage takes work," she said. "Supporting

each other's hopes and dreams. Listening and compromising. But wouldn't those things be easier with an emotional bond? Something powerful and all-consuming that keeps you together no matter how many curveballs life throws at you?"

The raw certainty in her eyes speared through him. A fervent crusader, she'd made a convincing argument for love. It might work on another man, one who hadn't seen the ravages of love up close and personal.

"And what happens when that powerful and all-consuming emotion dies?" he countered.

Hands on her hips, she pressed her lips together and glared at him. "I'll bet you think you're better off not letting anyone in. That way you don't get hurt. But isn't that awfully lonely? Don't you ever wish you could let someone take care of you for a change?"

And risk being disappointed when she stopped? "I'm a big boy," he said. "I haven't needed anyone for a long time."

She slipped the shirt over her head. "I'm sorry to hear that," she murmured and with one last searching glance, strode from the room.

Nathan threw off the sheet and stood, irrationally annoyed. He didn't need her pity. Or her love. He just needed her hand in marriage and her body in his bed.

Dismissing what felt suspiciously like regret, he headed for the shower.

Emma knelt on the floor, surrounded by the jewelry she'd made, and assessed a month's worth of work. Ten necklaces, a dozen pairs of earrings, fifteen rings and six bracelets. It wasn't enough. But it would have to do. In two days she was on her way to Baton Rouge for the art and design show. Her four weeks of exhausting work were at an end. This weekend would determine how the rest of her life would play out.

In the living room, Nathan sang along to a Sinatra tune.

The romantic music wrapped around her like a comfortable sweater and Emma found herself smiling. As much as she'd protested against moving into Nathan's condo, she had to admit that it had probably helped her prepare for the show. Left alone in her loft or staying at Addison's, she would have driven herself into the ground way before her deadline. Being forced to rest and eat, she'd met all her goals and crafted better jewelry. If she had a profitable show in Baton Rouge, she could credit a lot of that success to Nathan.

"So, this is where you've been hiding out." Addison appeared in the workroom doorway. She'd called an hour ago to say she was stopping by. "How is it going?"

"See for yourself." Emma gestured toward the pieces she'd recently finished.

Addison sat beside Emma and let her fingertips drift along a ruby-and-diamond necklace. "This is gorgeous."

"Here's the piece I created for the silent auction." Emma pulled a square flat box off her worktable and handed it to Addison. "I hope it makes up for the fact that I wasn't able to help you with the gala this year. I feel terrible about that."

For the last five years, she and Addison had co-chaired the committee in charge of a big event that raised money to fight juvenile diabetes. It was a labor of love for Addison, whose sister had been diagnosed with the disease at the age of five. How Addison managed a career, family and all her volunteer activities, Emma didn't have a clue. Her friend seemed tireless.

Emma was always happy to help, but this year her free time had been eaten up by her jewelry business and both her show and the gala fell on the same weekend.

"Don't worry about it," Addison said, popping the lid and gasping at the sparkling necklace that lay on the bed of black velvet. "This is incredible. And way more than you should be donating."

"You're sweet to say that. Here I was thinking I wasn't doing nearly enough."

The women hugged. Emma felt the burn of tears behind her eyes. She exhaled a shaky breath. Lately her emotions had been uncomfortably close to the surface. Frustration. Happiness. Desire. Anger. Emma's moods had been on a merry-go-round without end.

"I've missed having you around," Addison said. "But I can see why you decided to move in here."

"What are you talking about?" Emma stretched her lower back and grimaced as pain lanced through her muscles.

Addison eyed Emma. "You're sleeping with him, aren't you? Not that I blame you."

She wasn't ready to talk about how Nathan had swept her off to the bedroom every night for the last week or how the previous evening he'd plied her with a soothing massage that put her out for almost five hours. Damn the man.

As if her thoughts had conjured him, Nathan appeared in the doorway with a glass of wine he handed to Addison and a plate of cheese, bread and fresh fruit he placed on Emma's worktable.

"See if you can't persuade her to eat something," he said. "All her wonderful curves are disappearing."

Ever since she'd stopped making the trek to Addison's house every night, he'd been badgering her to eat and rest. After the first couple days, she'd stopped telling him that she could take care of herself. Why waste her breath when he wasn't listening to her anyway? And then three days ago, something awful had happened. She'd discovered that having him fuss over her was wonderful.

So much for Miss Independent.

"I'm not hungry," Emma said, frowning at him.

Tonight he wore a black T-shirt that clung to his chest and shoulders. The color emphasized the bad-boy gleam in his eyes and made her pulse hitch. All she wanted to do was lay her head against his broad chest and close her eyes.

"He won't stop fussing," Emma complained to Addison after he left. She popped a grape in her mouth and followed it up with a slice of Brie on fresh French bread. "It's not as if I need him to take care of me."

"But isn't it nice that he does?"

Addison's sly question hit a little too close to the mark. No one would believe Emma could take care of herself unless she demonstrated that she could. "I was doing okay before he came along."

Nathan returned with a glass of water for Emma. The ice cubes tinkled in the glass as he set it down. "Dinner will be ready in a half an hour. Can you stay?" he asked Addison.

Addison looked from one to the other. "I can't. I promised Paul I would be home for dinner tonight."

Emma watched him go, her gaze following his sexy posterior until it disappeared around the corner.

"For a woman who claims she's not interested, you are emitting some smoking-hot vibes." At least Addison waited until Nathan returned to the kitchen before her accusation burst forth. "I half expected to see scorch marks on his backside the way you were staring at him just now."

"It's awful." Emma massaged her stiff shoulders. "I can't stop myself. It's like handing a two-year-old a cookie and telling her not to eat it. He's impossible to resist."

"And given the way he looks at you, I think you'd better dust off your platinum card and buy yourself a trousseau. That man's got marriage on his mind."

Emma nodded. Pity that it was for all the wrong reasons.

Nathan covered his yawn with a fist as he parked Emma's borrowed van in the lot next to the Baton Rouge River Center. He blinked to bring moisture to his dry eyes. The clock on the dashboard told him it was a little before 9:00 p.m. Five hours earlier, he'd arrived home from a quick business trip to Chicago, anticipating a romantic reunion with the object of his desire and found her about to get behind the wheel of this dilapidated vehicle. Appalled by the idea that Emma intended to drive to Baton Rouge in something that had obviously seen more than its share of the open road, he'd overridden her objections and insisted on driving.

After the week he'd had, the last thing he'd wanted to do was more traveling. Not to mention that this was the worst possible moment for him to take time off. His brothers' interest in Lucas Smythe's company was taking on a life of its own. His location scouting near Chicago had not been as productive as he'd hoped. He really should be in the office tomorrow phoning Cody about other facility locations. What good would it do to win Emma and sign contracts with Silas if they had no production space?

Instead, he was in a van, almost three hundred miles away.

Nathan turned to the woman sleeping beside him. She'd napped almost the entire trip, confirming that he'd been absolutely right to insist on driving her to Baton Rouge. He'd never have forgiven himself if she'd fallen asleep at the wheel. And it wasn't as if his brothers would notice if he was out of the office another day.

She looked so peaceful. During the drive he'd contemplated how much he'd enjoy having her in his life on a permanent basis. Although he hadn't been blind to the perks of being married to Emma—the companionship, the incredible sex, the sense of purpose he'd felt these last ten days—he hadn't expected that she'd arouse such protectiveness in him, or that he would so completely enjoy something as simple as watching her sleep.

He liked taking care of her and sensed that as much as she resisted, she liked having him do so. Soon, she would realize they had all the elements for a solid marriage.

Everything but love.

The thought emerged out of the conversation with his father. Hearing Brandon praise Marissa for her strength and voice his regrets that he'd settled too fast into a marriage of convenience, Nathan had noticed doubt creep into his opinions on love. His father's words rang in his head, keeping him awake at night while Emma toiled down the hall, and forced him to notice a hole in his chest, a suspicion that something was missing.

Did he want Emma to love him the way his mother had loved Brandon? No, that couldn't be right. His mother's love hadn't made her happy. He wanted Emma to need him, lust for him, like him even. Nothing more. No unrealistic expectations mucking up what promised to be a satisfying blend of friendship and sex.

Nathan turned off the van and rubbed the back of his neck as he considered the woman asleep beside him. She'd lowered the seat back and turned on her side toward him. With one foot braced against the floor, she'd bent the other and her skirt rode halfway up her smooth thigh. He imagined running his hand up her leg until he reached heaven. He sighed. She was too tempting to be believed.

One hand pillowed her cheek. She'd draped the other across her middle. He reached out to grab her shoulder and shake her awake, but the soft skin beneath the denim jacket distracted him. Before he knew what he intended, Nathan slid his hand under the fabric and cupped the side of her neck, his thumb brushing her cheek. Mesmerized by the warmth and soft fragrance of her skin, he leaned down and swept his lips against hers.

Trapping a groan in his throat, he dipped his head again and lingered long enough to taste her. She stirred, her hand lifting to coast inside the open V of his cotton shirt. Placing her palm against his chest, her lips parted.

Nathan lost himself in the lazy press, slide and retreat of

his mouth against hers. He rubbed her lips with his, coaxing forth a soft murmur of delight. Her hand moved to the back of his neck, fingernails raking through his hair. Peace filled him. What was it about kissing Emma that made the world and his problems melt away?

Her perfume reminded him of springtime. He loved the season for all the possibilities it offered. The opportunity to build on past successes. A chance to grow in new directions. To take new risks.

Risks. In business. But not in his personal life.

Struck by the contrast, Nathan broke off the kiss. When it came to his heart, he shared his brothers' aversion to risk. It was the one way he didn't take after his father. Brandon had been bold in business *and* in love.

Memories surfaced. His father sitting on the worn couch in their tiny house, Marissa's feet in his lap. Marissa and Brandon washing dishes. Him kissing her neck. And laughter. Always laughter. His parents had been happy together, Nathan now realized. Devoted to each other. It wasn't being in love with his father that had made his mother unhappy. It had been their time apart that had hurt her. Funny how anger and resentment had tarnished his recollections of that.

Cupping Emma's face in his hands, he set his forehead against hers. "We're here."

"What time is it?"

"Close to nine. How long will it take you to set up?"

"A couple hours, I think."

"Are you hungry? We missed dinner. We could go grab something before getting started. You should probably keep your strength up."

"I'm too keyed up to eat. Maybe later, after we're done we could catch a late, late dinner." The hand that had been playing in his hair dropped to her lap. "Thanks for driving and letting me sleep."

"After almost a three-hour nap you probably won't feel

much like sleeping tonight," he said, kissing her brusquely on the forehead and setting her away from him. "I, on the other hand, feel like I could sleep for a week."

He caught the clear confusion on her face. The tender kiss they'd shared made him feel vulnerable in a way he'd never known with a woman. New insights into his parents' relationship made him question what he'd told Emma he wanted from her. He wasn't used to doubting his decisions. He wasn't used to feeling off balance.

He was no longer convinced that marrying without love was a good idea.

He just wasn't sure marrying for love was.

Nine

Emma half trotted to keep up with Nathan's long stride. She shot a glance at his profile, her chest tightening at the thoughtful frown pulling his brows together. He seemed miles away, and with longing tight and sharp beneath her skin, Emma felt all too present. What had just happened in the van?

Waking to the tenderness in his kiss had been her undoing. The memory of it yanked at her heart. His passion she could dismiss as lust and not let it into her soul, but gentleness—she had no protection against that.

In those seconds before he broke off the kiss, the last of her defenses crumbled to dust. Had Nathan noticed? Is that why he'd stopped kissing her? Did he realize that she'd lost the will to deny him? That he'd gotten her right where he wanted her?

She'd been working so hard this last week to keep her emotions separate from the incredible sex. It was getting harder and harder to resist the pull of longing that had nothing to do with how great he was in bed. She was hip-deep in trouble and sinking fast. Soon she'd enjoy being there.

Emma's hands clenched into fists, but there was no fighting the push and pull of excitement and anxiety that slid through her. She had to make enough money this weekend to escape the trap her father had laid for her. If Nathan was going to own her heart, she wanted to make sure he had to work for it. The only way to get on even footing with him was to take her father's meddling off the table. Being trussed up like a Christmas turkey and served to Nathan on a silver platter would put her at a distinct disadvantage.

Nathan was a silent, compelling presence beside her as she checked in with the show coordinator. With his help, she found her number on the poster board that displayed the layout of the show.

"I've got a great booth," she told Nathan, her finger on the square she would occupy for the next three days. "Look. It's on the main aisle and right in the middle of all the action."

Her enthusiasm must have been contagious because he grinned. "Let's go see it."

They struck out across the exhibition hall. Already most of the booths had been set up. An assortment of glass, pottery, metalwork, textiles, jewelry and wall art in a variety of mediums created a jumble of color and texture in the huge space. She'd been juried into this show and she knew the other artists here had been selected for their fine work as well. This was her first foray into the world of one-of-a-kind art, and her emotions overlaid one another, a hodgepodge of excitement and apprehension. So much rode on how she did here this weekend.

Emma slowed as she approached the space she'd been assigned. According to the map, her booth was on this corner. Instead of finding a blank slate, awaiting her personality and vision, the space contained a rather odd collection of sculptures depicting ugly old women in period clothing. On closer inspection, she saw they were made of small beads. While the detail impressed her, Emma couldn't quite get past the unattractive forms.

"Isn't this where you're supposed to be?" Nathan frowned as he surveyed what the area contained.

"Yes."

Her earlier excitement faded. Although she wanted the prime location, she couldn't bring herself to ask the artist to move his displays at this late hour. Disappointment seized her.

"Then he needs to move." Coiled energy radiated from Nathan.

She stepped between Nathan and the space she'd been assigned. "It's late. I don't want to be a bother."

"Don't be ridiculous. This is your booth. It's a great location. You should have it." His hard, gray gaze moved over her features and lingered on her worried frown. "Let me help you."

She closed her eyes to better resist his cajoling. "You've already done so much."

"You say that like it's a bad thing."

"It is." Her eyes flashed open. "I could get far too used to this."

"Then get used to it."

"I can't let myself. It's not who I am any longer. Not who I want to be."

Nathan wrapped her in a strong embrace, his breath warm against her temple as he sighed. "There's no reason you can't be independent and let me take care of you at the same time."

"Really? Because nothing you've done these past couple weeks has shown me that's true." She pushed against the unyielding wall of his chest. "Maybe if you stopped telling me what to do, I might let you take care of me a little."

Her tart speech had no effect on Nathan whatsoever.

He held her until her muscles loosened and she sagged against him. She liked letting him be her knight in shining armor. After a lifetime of being pampered, asserting her independence was hard work. Especially when she had a determined man tempting her to take it easy, to let her be spoiled.

But she'd be doing both of them a disservice if she meekly accepted what he offered and let him think it was enough to satisfy her.

"How about if I back off a little?" He pushed her to arm's length, his expression set into solemn lines. "Will that make you happy?" When she nodded, his grin flashed, smug and wicked. "Good. Now let me deal with this guy."

So much for him backing off.

He strode into the space, aiming straight at a young man with gel-spiked, short hair. "Excuse me. I think you've set up in the wrong spot. This space belongs to her."

The man shrugged. "She's late. I didn't think she was coming so I moved in." He turned his shoulder toward Nathan, clearly making the mistake of underestimating the tall, muscled man in faded jeans and casual white oxford shirt. "She can have my booth." He gestured to the empty space ten feet away.

"She doesn't want your space," Nathan said, his low voice firm, but polite. "She wants the booth she was assigned. This one."

"But I'm already set up here."

"But you don't belong here." Nathan pointed. "You belong there. Now, we're going out for dinner, and when we return, I expect that you will have vacated this booth."

He smiled, a slow, dangerous baring of teeth, and stepped toward the younger man. Although Nathan didn't make a single threatening movement, the other man's eyes widened, and he licked his lips nervously.

"Are we clear?"

"Yeah. Yeah, okay."

With a satisfied nod, Nathan pivoted on his heel and strode away, catching Emma's hand as he went. She turned to accompany him, knowing he would tow her along in his wake if she hesitated.

"What makes you think he'll move?" she demanded, her heart going all gooey at Nathan's demonstration of power and confidence.

He loosened his grip and slid his palm against hers, meshing their fingers. The warm, intimate clasp made her pulse dance.

The hard expression on his face melted into amusement as he glanced down at her. "He'll move."

She laughed breathlessly, warmed by the humor swirling in his eyes. "You can be very intimidating when you set your mind to it."

"Shall we stop by the show coordinator's table and point his transgression out to them?" he asked.

"Sure, maybe he'll move faster. Now that we're here I want to get everything set up."

He didn't relinquish her hand as they paused to mention their trouble to the coordinator. Nor did he let her go until he dropped a kiss on her knuckles and helped her into the van. Emma watched him through the windshield while he circled to his side and told her wayward hormones to behave. Avoiding the way he made her feel had been relatively easy while she'd been buried in her workroom, but she'd let her guard down with that fairy-tale wake-up kiss earlier and felt helpless against the pull of attraction between them.

"Are we going to sit down and eat or go to a drive-through?" he asked, starting the engine.

"Drive-through, but you knew that, didn't you?"

Nathan put the car in gear. "I suspected you'd want to get back as soon as possible."

* * *

On the second morning of the show, Emma sat opposite Nathan in the hotel restaurant and watched him tuck into a breakfast of steak and eggs. The man could certainly eat. Of course, he'd worked up an appetite last night after the show closed. She ducked behind the newspaper she'd bought, hiding a grin. The man could certainly make love, too.

Emma sipped coffee and nibbled on a piece of bacon. For the first time in weeks, her stomach wasn't churning from nervous tension. Maybe that was because, for the first time in weeks, a light had appeared at the end of the tunnel. The first day of the show had been surprisingly busy for a Friday. She'd made as much in one day as she'd made at Biella's in a month, and from what she'd gathered from the seasoned veterans at the show, she could look forward to the weekend being even busier.

"Look at this." Nathan reached out and snagged the paper from her hands and replaced it with a different section.

Emma stared in amazement at the huge photo of her necklace on the front of the entertainment section. "I can't believe it."

"I told you that reporter was going to do a piece on your jewelry," Nathan smirked.

"This is incredible publicity. Do you know what this means?"

"It means you'll be very busy today." Nathan signaled the waitress for their check. "And you owe me dinner. I'll provide dessert. I seem to recall that you like strawberries."

And what happened if she was busy? And successful beyond her wildest dreams? She'd thrown every bit of energy and focus into her jewelry, but until this instant, she hadn't truly believed it would save her. Now it looked very much as if it would.

That meant she would regain access to her money without having to marry Nathan. What were the chances that he'd stick around if he couldn't do the deal with her father? Would he disappear out of her life again?

"Do you want them dipped in chocolate or covered in whipped cream?" Nathan asked as he guided her out the door.

Emma blinked and shook her head. "What are you talking about?"

"Dessert. Strawberries. Chocolate or whipped cream?"

Laughter bubbled. "Since we're celebrating. How about both?"

Valentine's Day dawned overcast and cold. Nathan stood in his office and stared out the window at the rain falling on downtown Houston. The gray landscape was a complete contrast to his mood.

Ten days had passed since he and Emma had returned from Baton Rouge. The change in their relationship, sparked by that kiss in the van, continued to bemuse him. Never one to initiate their lovemaking, she now greeted him at the door each night, her ardent kisses providing the perfect appetizer.

Their time together, previously shadowed by mistrust and tension, had begun to approach the sort of domestic bliss his parents had enjoyed. He now understood why his father had always helped wash dishes even though the dishwasher functioned. Tangling with Emma's fingers in the soapy water had been both sexy and soothing for Nathan.

Neither one had brought up the topic of marriage. She kept mum about how she'd done at the show. A week went by. He was certain that he'd lost her. Lost the venture with Montgomery Oil.

When she'd first stated her intention to return the money to her account and thereby circumspect her father's plan to marry her off, Nathan had laughed at her efforts. Who would have guessed she had the talent to create such amazing jewelry or possessed the determination to work the long hours needed to get ready for the show?

The writeup in the paper had garnered her a great deal of attention. The traffic in her booth had been brisk. She'd charmed her customers with her salesmanship and dazzled them with her intricate jewelry. With each piece that disappeared out of the case, Nathan had seen his business deal with her father slipping through his fingers.

Then, a couple days ago, she'd admitted that she hadn't sold enough.

So Nathan knew she'd say yes when he popped the question tonight. She might prefer a marriage based on fanciful, unrealistic emotions instead of one built on respect and admiration, but she understood that what she needed was someone to take care of her.

The only thing that was still a mystery was whether his motivation for proposing remained the same as it had been six weeks ago, or if he'd decided he couldn't contemplate his future without her in it—business deal or no.

He shied away from the question, relieved that he'd never have to answer it. An hour ago, Sebastian had stopped by to say that Lucas Smythe needed a few more days to evaluate the offer he'd received from Case Consolidated Holdings. By this time tomorrow, Nathan would be engaged to Emma and his venture with Montgomery Oil secured.

"I've got a couple tickets to the Rockets that I can't use tonight. Interested?"

Nathan spied Max in the doorway. Although resentment still bubbled inside him at all the hoops his brothers were making him jump through, Nathan appreciated Max's attempt to reach out.

"Can't. Got plans."

"Me, too."

Max didn't leave Nathan's doorway. "Sebastian said he gave you the numbers for the Smythe purchase."

"I haven't had a chance to look them over yet."

"If you're still holding out for the Montgomery Oil deal, you're wasting your time. Chances are it's not going to happen."

"It will." Nathan's irritation rose, but he leashed his tone, striving for civility. "In fact, I'm set to close tonight."

"Have you really thought about what you're getting us into? We could stand to lose everything if the technology doesn't pan out." Max regarded him, his jaw jutting forward.

"Or we could stand to make a fortune."

"Is this really about the money, or are you just trying to destroy the family business?"

Long ago, after realizing that Sebastian and Max would never accept him as a brother, he'd put a cork in his frustration and decided that if he couldn't join them, he'd beat them. As alike as they were, he'd had no choice but to become an individual. Embedded habits were hard to break.

But at least *he* was trying.

"Do you really think I'd do that?" Nathan demanded, breathing hard. "Don't you see that I'm as much a part of this family and this business as you are? Of course you don't. You never let me be a part of anything you and Sebastian did. Frankly, I don't know why I'm busting my ass to bring this deal to Case Consolidated Holdings when I could do it on my own."

He stopped speaking, his hands clenching with the force of the rage that had risen up in him. The intensity of his emotions shocked him. He used to be cool under pressure. What had happened to the guy who bluffed professional gamblers with nothing but a two of hearts and a five of spades in his hand?

"So do the deal without us." Max shrugged. "You don't like it here anyway. I don't know why you don't just head out on your own."

This is exactly the sort of ultimatum he'd wanted to avoid

since returning to Houston and coming to work with his brothers. Max had tossed down the gauntlet.

"What's going on in here?" Sebastian entered the room and stood between Max and Nathan. He glanced from one brother to the other.

"Max doesn't seem to think I belong at this company," Nathan explained, unable to wrestle his bitterness to manageable levels. "And I'm starting to agree with him."

"Why is that?"

"I have a different vision for the company's future."

"And because you show up out of the blue—"

Nathan interrupted Max with a low growl. "I was brought in by Dad."

"So that gives you the right to push us to make changes. The company was profitable before you showed up. It will be profitable after you leave," Max shot back.

Around and around again with the same old arguments. The three of them could accomplish a hell of a lot more if they just stopped antagonizing each other.

Nathan pinched the bridge of his nose. "Look. We agreed that I'd have until today to get the deal done. If it doesn't happen, you'll never hear me mention Montgomery Oil again."

Valentine's Day had started out gray and overcast, but the sun had made an appearance by the time Emma let herself into Nathan's condo. She juggled three bags from expensive downtown boutiques and kicked the door closed. Shopping had never been less fun. Would she ever again spend money without thinking of all the hard work that went into earning it? She was no longer the overindulged girl she'd been six months ago. She'd learned the lesson that her father had intended.

Not that it mattered. Despite how well she'd done at the Baton Rouge show, she was almost $10,000 short of her goal. She'd screwed up her chance to prove to her father that she could support herself and lost the bet she'd made with him. Honor demanded that she marry Nathan.

Sure, she could renege and walk away a free woman. Losing her trust fund no longer bothered her. The last six weeks had demonstrated that she could take care of herself. But she'd like her word to count for something. And if she'd won and her father lost, she'd expect him to live up to his end of the bargain. She could do no less.

As to how she felt about becoming Mrs. Nathan Case…

Emma stripped off her clothes and stepped beneath the shower, her thoughts locked on Nathan. On the long drive back from Baton Rouge, she'd had lots of time to think. Since moving in with him, some shift in her perception had occurred.

As hot water cascaded over her body, she shut her eyes and imagined his hands roving over her, his long, muscular frame sliding against her bare skin, awakening her desires, his deep voice crooning encouragement as they moved together. He did things to her body she'd never experienced before.

And he made her happy. He took care of her needs both in and out of bed. Feeling cherished and fussed over had opened the door to her considering Nathan's opinions about marriage. She'd learned enough about him in the last couple weeks to decide that he'd make a great husband. He was committed to their relationship and concerned about her needs.

Still, she knew passion would never be enough for her. But what if it was combined with respect and affection? Emma wasn't sure. Marriages failed even when the couple loved each other. Could she and Nathan make it without a strong emotional bond?

Emma exited the shower and dried her hair. It was Valentine's Day. Her day of reckoning. Although Nathan hadn't mentioned the deal with her father since they'd returned from Baton Rouge, she knew he was gearing up for a romantic evening with a marriage proposal at its core.

Was it reasonable to surmise that she could continue to be happy with Nathan, knowing he would resist losing his heart to her? He sang joyful songs of love and forever, but he didn't believe a single word. Yet each chorus, every verse spoke to her, seduced her into believing that he could fall in love if he found the right woman.

And more than anything, she longed to be that right woman.

Her heart stopped. Something inside her clicked into place. The final piece of a puzzle that made the picture whole.

No wonder she was considering marrying him when she'd determined from the first that she wanted a fairy-tale ending. That she deserved to marry a man who adored her.

She loved Nathan.

What she'd feared would happen had come to pass. She'd fallen for him. Hard. And Nathan wasn't ready to let her in. To love her. He might never be. Was she really prepared to settle for that?

Her cell phone rang. She plucked it from her purse and answered it.

"Are you done with your errands?"

Despite the long hours spent stretched out in bed beside him, beneath him, on top of him the previous evening, hearing Nathan's voice awakened that familiar ache in her body.

"All done."

"Can you meet me in an hour?"

"What did you have in mind?" Despite her somber mood a moment ago, salacious thoughts began a slow striptease in her head. It did no good to wallow in misery when just talking to Nathan aroused her.

"I had been thinking about lunch, unless you had a little afternoon delight in mind."

"Why couldn't we do both? Surely there's a hotel some-where nearby your office that offers room service." A picture formed in her mind. She took a moment and savored the fantasy while Nathan's voice rumbled in her ear.

"Are you listening to me?"

"No, sorry. I was mentally undressing you. What was that you were saying?" she asked.

A muffled curse filled her ear. "Pack a bag. I've booked a suite at the Four Seasons."

"I'm on my way."

Emma ended the call and touched her lips, fingertip gliding from one end of her wide grin to the other. She should be worried that the man made her wild with anticipation after just a phone call. He was a heartbreak ready to happen, but she'd promised herself no more worrying about the future. Just live in the moment.

Easier said than done, but an hour later she strolled into the hotel lobby and spotted Nathan. He sat on one of the comfortable couches, reading the newspaper and looking every inch the corporate executive. For a moment she stopped and stared at him, her heart pounding.

Gone was her sexy seducer in jeans and bare chest. In a custom-tailored navy suit with a crisp white shirt and butter-yellow silk tie, he'd become a tycoon once more. The exact sort who'd be in business with her father. Her heart hit her toes.

Nathan looked up and caught her staring at him. His eyebrows rose slowly, giving her blood a chance to heat. The lazy smile that followed became her undoing.

"Hello, handsome," she said, sauntering over on shaky legs to sit beside him on the couch. She angled her body toward him and crossed one leg over the other, trying her best to look seductive. She'd worn an emerald-green sheath that skimmed her curves and bared her arms. "Come here often?"

His gaze toured her ankles and calves before taking in the rest of her Dior-clad body. By the time he reached her face, she buzzed with desire. He folded the paper and used it to tap her bare knee.

"Obviously not often enough if you represent their clientele. I have a suite reserved. Could I interest you in a drink?"

"While that sounds lovely, I'm afraid I'm waiting for my lover. We rendezvous every Thursday at one. He is very handsome and very sexy."

"And very late. It is already five minutes after one." Nathan flicked his cuff over his watch and his lips curved in a his-loss-my-gain smile. "Have a drink with me. A man should never keep a beautiful woman waiting."

"Well, since you put it that way."

Emma laughed as Nathan pulled her to her feet.

He sent a bellboy to fetch her things. In the suite, while Nathan tipped the man and sent him on his way, Emma pulled out the room service menu and flipped through it. Nathan came to stand behind her, his fingers grasping the zipper at her nape.

"Hungry?" He slid the zipper down her back and bent to kiss her shoulder.

Emma turned in his arms, letting the dress fall to her feet. "Dessert first."

Wrapped in a plush towel provided by the hotel, Emma dried her hair and regarded her reflection. Her eyes sparkled with secret delight and an irrepressible smile lifted the corners of her mouth. She glowed the way a woman who'd spent the afternoon being the object of a man's adoring caresses ought to. Thank goodness it wasn't illegal to feel this wonderful.

Just thinking about the exquisite way Nathan had plied her body made her shiver anew at the realization that they had all night to indulge in more such perfect loving. Of course, if they continued at their current pace, she might be dead of exhaustion by morning. But what a way to go.

"What are you thinking about?" Nathan returned from the

bedroom where he'd been ordering room service. He stepped behind her and met her gaze in the mirror.

"You," she replied, her smile turning salacious. "On the dining table in the other room, covered in whipped cream and chocolate sauce."

His brows rose. "I think it's your turn." His hands snaked around her waist to loosen the robe's belt.

"We can't," she protested, turning off the hair dryer so she could clutch the robe closed. "Dinner first. I've got to eat to keep my strength up."

"You don't need strength for what I have in mind. Just lie back and let me do all the work." His grin was pure wolf.

She laughed, but continued to defend herself from his questing hands. Breathless with rising desire and from resisting his efforts to separate her from the robe, she was only half-relieved when a knock on the door announced room service.

While Nathan went to let the waiter in, Emma quickly checked her voice mail. She was hoping for a call from a woman who'd been interested in commissioning a piece of jewelry from her. Granted, it was too late for her to use the money toward winning the wager with her father, but this sort of business would provide a whole new source of income.

She wondered how Nathan would take the news that she intended to keep designing and producing jewelry after they married. He'd told her over and over that he wanted to take care of her, but she'd proved that she could take care of herself. She was proud of the business she'd started and the success she'd had. She had no intention of giving it up because she no longer needed the money she made from it.

Two messages had come in during the afternoon. One from Addison, wishing her good luck on her evening with Nathan. The second was from Thomas McCann at Biella's. She'd called him earlier, hoping against hope that he'd had some luck selling the pieces that hadn't sold at the Baton

Rouge show. He'd been out, so she'd had to leave a message. Crossing her fingers, she listened.

"Emma, I'm glad you called. I have good news. We've sold all the new stuff you brought us. The buyers mentioned seeing your work at a recent charity event. I have a check for almost $11,000 waiting for you. And we'd really like it if you'd bring us more of your jewelry."

In stunned disbelief, Emma ended the call. She set the phone on the dresser, scarcely able to wrap her head around what she'd heard. She'd done it. She'd met her goal by the deadline.

She would get her trust fund back. She could remodel her loft. Buy new equipment. Secure studio space. Market her designs and grow her business.

She was no longer obligated to marry Nathan.

Emma's stomach muscles clenched in distress.

She loved Nathan. She might not have come to terms with marrying a man who couldn't or wouldn't love her, but she'd accepted that she was going to honor the bet with her father.

Now everything was different. She was free to choose whether or not to marry Nathan.

In some ways, things had gotten much worse. Free will left her wide open to mistakes.

Before coming here tonight, she'd accepted that he didn't love her and had grown accustomed to the idea of marrying him anyway. No, more than that, a part of her wanted to be his wife. She couldn't imagine living without him.

But if she followed her heart and married him, would she eventually grow dissatisfied and spend the rest of her life angry at herself and resenting him? All she needed was some sign, some admission, that his feelings for her were stronger than affection.

And if he didn't love her? Was she prepared to walk away?

She stared around the bedroom. Nathan had staged the

perfect romantic scene with roses, candles and chocolate-covered strawberries. She took in the unmade bed, where they'd spent the afternoon in sensual decadence, and the red roses on the dresser.

Instead of opening into full blossoms, the buds drooped on their sturdy stems. Emma knew the flowers were dying. They'd looked so beautiful, so perfect this afternoon when she and Nathan had first entered the lavish suite. But their loveliness had been an illusion. They were never going to last.

Was that a sign that she and Nathan weren't going to last, either?

Ten

Wondering what could be keeping Emma, Nathan reentered the bedroom and found her standing, lost in thought. Taking her by the hand, he drew her into the suite's main room, where dinner awaited. Candlelight sparkled off the cut-crystal glassware and highlighted the gold pattern on the china.

Nathan pulled out a chair and Emma sat down. His heart bucked as he knelt beside her chair, but other than that, he felt remarkably calm. This was the moment he'd been anticipating all day. "I have something for you." Still holding her hand, he turned her palm up. "Marry me."

Silence filled the room while Emma stared at a magnificent diamond glittering on her palm. Despite the uncertainty in her eyes, her lips twitched. "Most men propose with a ring."

"I figured you'd rather design your own."

"You'd be right."

"You haven't answered my question," he prompted.

She closed her fingers, trapping the diamond in her fist. "Funny, I didn't hear a question." She raised her chin and met his gaze. The hope and wariness at war in her dark brown eyes didn't ease the tightness in his chest. "It sounded more like a demand."

And it had been. Nathan immediately recognized his mistake. She was a fanciful girl who believed in fairy tales. He'd offered her practicality. He turned over the hand clenched around the diamond and dusted a reverent kiss across her knuckles. "Emma Montgomery, will you marry me?"

"Can you promise me I'll never regret it?"

"No."

At last she smiled. But it was a pale representation of true happiness. "You could have lied and told me yes."

"I'd rather be honest with you." He cupped her face in his hands. "I want our marriage to be based on respect and trust."

"But if there was no deal with my father you wouldn't be marrying me."

"Deal or no deal, if I didn't want to marry you, I wouldn't."

An intense light entered her eyes. Her whole body vibrated with tension. "Do you think you could ever love me?"

Here was the question he'd been dreading. The businessman in him counseled lying to her, but that would mean he would spend the rest of his life living a sham. He needed to be truthful, even if he risked losing her.

"I can't promise you a happily-ever-after, but you'll never question my commitment to you or our life together." He released her chin to coast a gentle caress against her cheek. "Marry me."

She deflated beneath his words. "I don't have to."

"What do you mean?" he demanded.

"My jewelry sold at Biella's. It's enough to replace all the money in my account. I won the bet with my father." Her voice shook. "I no longer have to settle for a marriage based only on trust and respect."

"You want love." He dragged his hand though his hair. A muscle ticked in his jaw.

"More than anything." Her warm chocolate eyes cooled as his scorn struck her.

"There is no such thing as a fairy-tale ending, Emma."

"Not for us," she whispered. "Not if you can't love me. But maybe someday for me if I don't marry you."

"You're a fool."

She pushed his hands away and stood. "No, I'm not."

Nathan got to his feet as well, but slowly, uncoiling one muscle at a time while he fought to keep his frustration in check. "You'll spend the rest of your days chasing rainbows only to have them fade before you catch them. That's what love is. An illusion."

"You're wrong. Love is what keeps us together through the worst life throws at us. It's hope and faith. It makes us strong. And you'd see that if you'd just stop expecting to be disappointed."

"You're the one who's wrong if you think I don't feel something for you."

"Not love—" She gasped as he caught her upper arms and pulled her flush against him.

A long silence followed her statement, punctuated only by their ragged breathing. Despite being angry with her, desire sank long talons into him. He could take her to bed and make love to her until she stopped thinking. He'd bring her to the edge of orgasm over and over until she admitted that he was the only man she would ever belong to like that.

But eventually they would have to leave the bed and the arguments would begin all over again. He wouldn't compromise, and neither would she. Round and round with no hope that either one would bend.

"I guess we're at an impasse then," he said. His hands fell away. She'd gotten what she wanted. She had no reason to marry him, which made his deal with her father null and void.

He had nothing more to fight for. "I hope you don't regret this decision."

Emma turned her back to him, but not before he saw her mouth twist into a grim line. "Why would I?"

"Because with me, for better or worse, you know exactly what you get. Will you be so sure of the next guy?"

When she didn't answer, Nathan retreated to the bedroom to gather his things. He dressed quickly and came to stand before her. She hadn't moved while he was packing, but now, her hand lifted toward his sleeve.

Before she touched him, he spoke. "Goodbye, Emma."

He gave the words a ring of permanence. He wanted her to understand that he was leaving her for good. No turning back.

"Goodbye, Nathan. Be happy."

Snarling at her parting words, he walked out of the hotel suite and out of her life.

The second half of February was busy for Emma. Unenthusiastic about tackling the major remodeling job it needed, she put her loft up for sale, marketing it as is, and moved her things into a tiny two-bedroom apartment. With her jewelry selling well at Biella's, she expanded into a couple stores in Dallas and Austin. Losing herself in work might not be a cure for heartbreak, but driving herself to exhaustion was a boon to her jewelry inventory.

Nathan never showed up at her door. She wasn't surprised. She'd refused to marry him. His deal with her father was done. So he was done with her.

She forced herself to eat even though her stomach protested at the mere thought of food. Every morning as she brushed her teeth, she confronted her ghost in the mirror. If she'd had the energy, she would have laughed at the contrast between the glowing, animated woman she'd been at Nathan's condo and the shadowy creature she'd become.

But nights were the worst. Questions haunted her. Had refusing Nathan been the right thing to do? Was a lifetime of heartache worth her self-respect? Did he think of her? She wanted to marry for love. By standing up for what she believed in, she'd gained her self-respect and lost her heart.

Only time would tell if she'd made the right choice.

March rolled in, bringing sunshine and warmer temperatures. A day came when Emma dressed in jeans and her favorite purple blouse and went shopping. She needed groceries and one special item.

An hour later, Emma stood in her bathroom and stared at the pregnancy test in her hand. The instructions on the box said the test was ninety-nine percent accurate, but Emma wanted to be absolutely positive—scratch that, confident about the results.

What if she was pregnant?

Horrified brown eyes stared back at her from the mirror.

Pregnant with Nathan's baby.

After the way he'd walked out on her, she knew he never wanted to hear from her again. A pregnancy would bring him back into her life. What would that mean?

She took the test, set the stick on the toilet tank, and left the bathroom in a daze. She needed to talk to someone, and with Addison out of town, she picked up the phone and dialed her sister-in-law, Jaime.

"Hi, stranger," Jaime said. "Haven't heard from you lately."

"I've been sort of busy. How are you feeling?"

"I'll be better in a week when the baby comes. Ouch. He's active today. Lately he gets restless at night."

Emma lifted her shirt and fanned her fingers over her still-flat midsection. She stared at her navel.

Was she going to be a mother?

"I had hoped to be in our new house before he was born, but it's not going to work out," Jaime continued. "I can't wait to get out of here. Living with your father means living where there's no privacy and no peace. He tells Cody what to do about everything. It drives me crazy. I don't know why I let that husband of mine talk me into moving in here while our house was being built. We'd have been better off in a hotel."

"I'm sure the maid service isn't nearly as good at the Lancaster as it is at Chateau Montgomery."

"True, but at least I could have my husband to myself." Jaime continued her one-sided conversation, then must have noticed she no longer had an audience. "Emma, are you okay?"

"I think I'm pregnant."

"Pregnant?"

Emma winced as Jaime's voice shrilled in her ear.

"Emma, pregnant? Are you sure?"

"No, I'm not sure. I'm taking the test right now. And could you please keep your voice down?"

"Is it Nathan's baby?" Jaime whispered. "Of course it is. Are you going to marry him now?"

"No."

Being pregnant didn't change anything between them. He still didn't love her. But it gave her an excuse to lie to herself and say that no longer mattered. She was pregnant with his child. An illegitimate child. It had been hard for Nathan to grow up an outsider in his father's household. Would he let his son suffer the same way?

"How long has it been since you took the test?"

Glancing at her watch, she realized that time was up. Emma raked an unsteady hand through her long hair. "About ten minutes."

"Go check."

Emma retraced her steps to the bathroom. She picked up the stick and closed her eyes. With a deep breath gathered in her lungs, she looked at the pregnancy test.

"Positive." Emma sat down on the bathroom floor. "I'm pregnant."

"I'm sure he'll be thrilled." Jaime's tone rang with conviction. "Cody said Nathan's had a thing for you for years."

Hope curled around Emma like a snake, slowly strangling her good sense. "If by *thing* you mean he wanted to get me into bed, then I agree. I know I'd be wasting my breath to ask you to keep this from your husband. But please tell Cody not to say anything to Nathan. I need to figure out what I'm going to do. And for heaven's sake, make sure he doesn't tell Daddy."

"Call me later in the week and tell me how you're doing."

"I will."

"And if you need anything, you know Cody and I will be here for you."

Tears pricked Emma's eyes. "Thanks."

"Sorry to interrupt your meeting." Missy, Sebastian's executive assistant, stuck her head through the door and smiled in apology. "But I thought you should know that Cody Montgomery is here to see Nathan."

Sebastian and Max looked at each other then locked their gazes on Nathan. "I thought you told Montgomery Oil that we passed," Sebastian said.

"I'm sure it's a social call."

"Social?" Max demanded. "Since when are you so cozy with the Montgomerys?"

"Since Cody and I went to college together."

"That's why you were so damn confident you'd get to do the deal. You had an in with the old man."

Annoyance briefly flared at Max's accusation. Then, Nathan shrugged. Why bother defending himself? Let his brothers think what they wanted. Nothing held any appeal for him these days—not besting his brothers, not making money, not even the opportunity to purchase an Onderdonk painting he'd wanted for ten years. Since he'd walked out on Emma, all roads led to regret.

Nathan lifted his feet off the coffee table and strode out of the room. Lately, everything fed his restless streak, from his brothers' uninspired decisions about the business, to sitting in his office where nothing stirred his interest, to going home to his empty condo.

He hated his life. It was lonely, dull and he'd never been more miserable. He'd failed to impress his brothers with his business savvy. In fact, he'd further aggravated his relationship with them by being surly and distant for the last two weeks. And he'd turned his back on the most amazing woman he'd ever met. He deserved to be miserable.

He found Cody pacing the lobby. "What are you doing in Houston?"

"I met with a couple of our board members this morning, but we got done early and I wondered if you had time for lunch before I head back."

Nathan glanced at his watch. "The restaurant downstairs doesn't open for another twenty minutes. Are you sure you have time to hang out in Houston? Isn't your wife due any day now?"

"We've got a couple days to go." Cody grimaced. "Although she'd probably be happy if it happened sooner." He glanced around and noticed the paintings on the wall. "Hey, those look like the ones Dad has in his office."

"Onderdonk." Nathan nodded, wondering what was up with the Montgomery family and his art collection.

"I thought so. I think Emma got him to buy them. And speaking of my sister, what's going on with you two?"

Cody's blunt transition from paintings to Emma warned Nathan that this wasn't a casual visit. "Let's go talk in my office." He gestured down the hall. "Nothing is going on between us."

The look Cody shot him reminded Nathan of Emma. Pain

lanced through him. He didn't want to hurt. When his mother died, he'd sworn never to let himself yield to loving anyone again. Yet Emma had wriggled her way beneath his guard and he'd begun to open his heart to her.

"Any reason you can't pick up the phone and see if she's all right?" Cody's aggressive tone caught Nathan by surprise.

Had something bad happened to Emma? No, if it had, Cody would have led with that.

"The last time we spoke, she made it pretty clear she doesn't want to hear from me."

"You might be wrong about that."

Nathan's spirits perked up. "Did she say that?"

"I haven't spoken with her."

"Then how do you know she wants to hear from me?"

"She and Jaime talk. Jaime talks to me." Cody shot him a dark look. "You need to talk to Emma."

Nathan didn't know what to make of his friend's sharp tone. "What you're saying makes no sense."

They passed Sebastian's office, and Nathan caught his brothers watching them with keen interest.

He gestured Cody into his office. "What's going on?"

Cody glanced pointedly at the open door until Nathan shut it. "Dad's not giving Emma back her trust fund."

Nathan's gut tightened as he pictured her living in her half-renovated condo. She deserved better than that.

"Why?"

"Because she didn't marry you."

Remorse twisted in Nathan's gut like a meal of bad shellfish. "I don't understand. She told me she had the hundred thousand she needed."

"But apparently she needed to have it back in her account by the fourteenth and it wasn't there until the next day."

"Ridiculous." Nathan shook his head. "She had the money. So what if it wasn't in some account?"

"That's the old man." Cody shrugged. "And speaking of

the old man, he said that the deal's still good if you marry Emma."

All at once Nathan realized that he wasn't interested in the venture with Montgomery Oil because he no longer wanted to take the business away from his brothers. He wanted to be in business with his brothers. He wanted to be accepted as part of the family.

"She already said no."

"Perhaps you went about it the wrong way," Cody countered.

Nathan crossed his arm over his chest. "Perhaps I did."

There was no *perhaps* about it. Emma needed the sort of fairy-tale romance he couldn't give her. She hadn't been happy with his passion and promises of fidelity. She wanted him to love her. She thought that would make her happy. Ridiculous. Love only led to disappointment and heartache. Look how his mother had suffered as the mistress of a man who would never truly be hers. Look at how he'd been ostracized by his brothers. Look what trying to be accepted by them had done to his life. Love wouldn't make anyone happy.

"Try asking her again. Things are a little different for her these days."

"Because she's broke?"

Cody stared at Nathan like he was the biggest idiot on the planet. "Because she's pregnant."

"Pregnant?" Nathan echoed. The floor shifted beneath his feet. "Are you sure?"

"As sure as a pregnancy test can be." Cody put his hand on Nathan's arm. "You look like you need to sit down."

Nathan dropped into a chair. "Emma's pregnant? Why didn't she tell me?"

"I figured she had."

Nathan pinned his best friend with a hot glare. "And you thought I wasn't going to do the right thing by her?"

Cody shrugged, but before he could defend himself against

Nathan's accusation, his cell phone rang. While Cody took the call, Nathan leapt from the chair and began to pace.

How long had Emma known she was pregnant? Why hadn't she called or come by to let him know he was about to be a father?

A father. Nathan was lightheaded with relief.

He stared at the art on his walls. He and Emma were permanently linked now. She would marry him. He wasn't going to give up until she agreed. No child of his was going to grow up illegitimate.

"Looks like I don't have time for lunch after all," Cody said. "Jaime's water just broke. You've got to talk to my sister."

"Tell me something I don't know," Nathan muttered.

After Cody left, Nathan grabbed his car keys and headed for the elevator. He got no farther than Sebastian's office.

"What did he want?" Max demanded, stepping into the hall and blocking Nathan's path.

"He came to have lunch."

"That's it?" Sebastian stepped from his office and exchanged a glance with Max.

Their nonverbal communication grated on Nathan. He wrestled with the resentment that had become such a part of him and the revelation that he wanted to work *with* Max and Sebastian instead of against them. But how was he going to make that happen when they shut him out? They'd always had each other. They didn't need him. Disappointment made him surly.

"And to deliver a message that Silas is still interested in going forward."

"We've already decided that we're out," Max said.

"I've got some friends who would jump at the chance to get in on this with me."

Sebastian looked disappointed. "Are you considering it?"

"Any reason why I shouldn't?" He looked from one to the other.

"Is that what you want?" Max demanded, frowning.

"I thought you came back to Houston because you wanted to work with us," Sebastian added.

"And you sure haven't made that easy for me, have you?" Nathan shot back and abruptly ran out of steam. "Truth is, I'm no longer interested in working with Montgomery Oil."

"Why not?" Sebastian asked.

"I came back to Houston because I wanted to be a part of this company, a part of this family." He gave the last word a bitter jab. "Ever since we were kids you two have been in a club I could never join. After Dad called and asked me to come back and join the company, for the sake of family, I let you two shoot down every idea I had. I figured that eventually you'd get over whatever problem you had with me and realize that I know what I'm doing. The venture with Montgomery was my chance."

Sebastian gestured with his head toward Max. "And we stopped it from happening."

Max shrugged before saying, "Maybe we've misjudged you a bit."

"We've let pride get in the way of family," Sebastian added.

For the first time since returning to Houston, Nathan had a glimmer of hope that what he'd come back to find might be within reach. A powerful emotion swept him, locked up his chest and made him want to grin like an idiot. "I'm willing to work together if you are."

"Smythe is waffling," Sebastian said. "If this venture with Montgomery Oil is still on the table, I think we should go for it."

Nathan shook his head. He no longer had anything to prove to his brothers and everything to prove to Emma. "Let's hang in there with Smythe. The company is solid. It's exactly what we need to diversify our holdings. Lucas will come around."

"You sure this is what you want?" Sebastian asked.

"I wouldn't have it any other way."

Eleven

Armed with one of Nathan's dress shirts that she'd *accidentally* packed when she'd left his condo, Emma stepped off the elevator into the lobby of Case Consolidated Holdings. Since moving out on her own, she'd taken to wearing it to bed at night, comforted by the familiar cologne that clung to the cotton. Newly laundered, it no longer contained his scent.

She missed him.

Ached for him.

Had it only been two weeks since Valentine's Day? It felt like a year.

Emma's polite smile for the receptionist faded as the woman told her Nathan wasn't in. Relief and disappointment tumbled through her. She'd been preparing for this meeting for a couple days, running a hundred different speeches through her mind, even practicing a few in front of the mirror.

In the end, it all came down to, "Nathan, I'm pregnant."

Funny. It didn't get easier with repetition.

"Do you want to leave him a message?" the receptionist asked with a bright smile.

"Did he say when he was going to be back?" Now that she'd summoned the courage to tell him, she wanted to get it over with. "Maybe I could wait."

"He didn't say."

"I'll try back later." Unless she talked herself out of it.

Earlier, when she'd organized her day, she'd planned to stop at Biella's first because they'd called to say a check awaited her, but once she'd parked, she'd been overcome with the need to see Nathan and had selected this daunting errand to run first. Now she'd have to get up the nerve to make this journey all over again.

Anxiety snacked on her poise as she returned to the elevator. Before she could press the down button, the door opened and Emma found herself staring into Nathan's eyes.

"What are you doing here?" he demanded.

All her carefully prepared greetings evaporated as her stomach flipped like a frisky dolphin. She shoved the shirt she held toward him.

"I brought you back your shirt. It got mixed up in some of my things, and I packed it by accident."

"And you made a special trip to deliver it." His voice took on the sexy rumble that always had her out of her clothes in record time. "I'm glad."

Nathan took the shirt and tossed it onto one of the nearby lobby chairs. Then, he slid his fingers around her arm and pulled her into the elevator. His free hand coasted over her hip and in one smooth move, he pinned her between the wall and his lean muscles.

Giddy with delight at being crushed against his rock-solid frame, she put her hand on Nathan's chest, feeling the steady, soothing thrum of his heart.

"It was no bother. I was in the neighborhood."

"And here I was looking everywhere for you," he said.

Beneath Nathan's intense regard, Emma's cheeks heated. Then her blood. "You were? Why?"

"I've missed you."

Emma's nerves began to purr. She half closed her eyes and peered at him from beneath her lashes. Although she longed to hear a different set of three words from Nathan, these ran a close second. Was it possible that he felt something more for her than simple lust? Could his emotions be more complex than she thought?

"Not enough to call." She reached deep for a breezy smile and found one. No reason he had to know how heavy her heart had become.

He stroked a strand of her hair off her cheek. "You made it clear that we were done."

She'd made it clear? "You walked out on me, remember?"

"I was a fool to do that."

"But you did. What's changed?"

"We're meant to be together. Don't you feel it?"

Did that mean he loved her? Was it possible? Breathless with hope, she lifted onto her toes. As his lips covered hers in a slow, coaxing kiss, Emma dug her fingers into his back and stopped fighting his web of sensual entanglement. Beneath his intoxicating kisses, it was easy to let the last two weeks, and all her heartache, become a vague memory.

For so long, she'd fought to keep from losing herself in him, fearing he would never feel the same way about her. But he was so hard to resist, and she'd slipped further beneath his spell. It had taken all her willpower not to confess, over and over again, that she loved him. She could no longer fight what was in her heart.

"I love you," she said when his lips eased off hers. Once the truth came out, admitting the rest seemed inevitable. "I have for a long time."

"But you won't marry me."

Was marriage even on the table?

"I thought the deal with my father fell through."

"It did."

Her heart swelled with joy, but she remained cautious. "Then there's no reason for you to want to marry me."

"There are lots of reasons," he said, but as the elevator gently decelerated and the doors opened, he left them unvoiced.

Taking her by the hand, Nathan towed her past the crowd waiting to get on the elevator and into the office building's big, bright lobby. With her emotions a melting pot of worry and glee, she was only half aware of the voices, laughter and clink of dishes that echoed through the two-story atrium.

"Let's go to lunch," he said.

One of downtown Houston's best restaurants occupied the open space and drew large crowds to sample the widely reviewed cuisine. Emma balked. She wasn't eager to confide in Nathan about her pregnancy in a crowded restaurant.

"I have an errand to run. How about we meet in an hour?"

Nathan shook his head. "Now that I have you, I'm not letting you go. We'll run your errand together, and then I'll take you to lunch."

"Somewhere quiet?"

"Anywhere you want."

They headed outside. After days of rain, the sun had decided to make a brief appearance. Emma savored the warmth against her skin and inhaled the scent of dampness that clung to the pavement and plants. Nathan laced their fingers as they strolled along the sidewalk, his presence a solid, dependable strength by her side. She curled up in the crook of his arm and leaned her head against his shoulder.

For the first time in weeks she felt happy.

"Where are we heading?" he asked.

"Biella's. I'm bringing more of my jewelry for them to sell."

At the word *jewelry,* Nathan lifted their clasped hands and grazed his lips against her bare ring finger. "Did you ever make your engagement ring?"

She thought of the black, velvet-lined box in her purse. "Why bother when there is no engagement?"

Despite her tart tone, he grinned at her. "Can I see it?"

Was she really that transparent? Heaving a sigh, she fished out the ring box and dropped it into his outstretched hand. He popped it into his pocket without opening it. Emma's heart thundered and vertigo struck her again. She must have wavered because Nathan stopped and turned her to face him.

"Are you all right?" He cupped her cheek, thumb stroking her skin in a soothing rhythm. The concern shadowing his eyes made her long to rest her head against the powerful expanse of his chest.

Instead, she grabbed his hand and pulled it away from her cheek. "I'm fine. Just a little dizzy from not eating breakfast this morning."

"We should have stopped for lunch first."

"Biella's is right there." She pointed to the store. "This will only take a second."

As they waited for a sales clerk to get the manager, Nathan surveyed her jewelry. "There's not much here."

Thinking that he didn't recognize her older designs, Emma peered into the case. Delight seized her as she counted. Another five pieces had sold.

Thomas McMann appeared across the case from them, smiling. "Ms. Montgomery, how nice that you came by. As you can see, your designs are in high demand." He handed her an envelope containing her check. "I hope you brought us some more of your work."

"I have these." Emma pulled from her bag the newest pieces she'd created.

"And there's this." Nathan placed the ring box on the counter.

Before Emma could stop him, Thomas McMann snatched the box and opened it. He smiled with delight. "This is lovely. Do you have more engagement designs? I do a lot of wedding business. White gold or platinum?"

"Platinum. But it's not for sale." She shot Nathan a sour look.

He responded with a shrug. "I don't see why not. You're not going to wear it. You might as well sell it and make some money."

Emma met the challenge in Nathan's gaze and grappled for something to say.

"Unless, of course, you've changed your mind about marrying me."

"Why would I do that?" She sounded breathless and as uncertain as she felt.

She'd come to his office today, knowing he wouldn't want his child growing up without a father, and willing to marry him for that reason. But in the elevator, she'd started to think that maybe he'd fallen in love with her a little. In fact, in the space of a few heartbeats, she'd pinned all her hopes and dreams on it. She searched his expression for some sign that she'd been right.

"I thought maybe something had changed."

All at once it hit her. Sparkling lights appeared before her eyes. She flushed hot from head to toe. "You know."

"Know what?"

She didn't buy his innocent act for a second. He knew she was pregnant. That's why he wanted to marry her. Not because he was starting to love her.

Awash in dismay, Emma gripped the counter, mortified to realize that Thomas McCann watched their exchange with obvious curiosity. She blinked, mustered a polite smile and scooped up her engagement ring.

"I'll bring by some wedding sets next week. I think you'll love the designs. Have a nice day."

With that, she shot Nathan a hard look, pivoted on her heel and marched out of the store. Annoyance fueled her pace, and she reached the sidewalk before he caught up with her.

What a fool she was.

"Slow down." Nathan touched her arm, but she shook him off. "Where are you going?"

Where was she heading? For a moment Emma couldn't recall where she'd parked her car. Frustration made her grind her teeth. How could she shake Nathan and go lick her wounds in private if she couldn't find her car? A lump blocked her throat. She swallowed, but it wouldn't go away.

"Emma, please talk to me."

She shook her head.

"Let's go have lunch."

She shook her head again.

"You have to eat. It's important to keep up your strength."

She stopped dead in her tracks. "You know I'm pregnant." Emma pointed at him in warning as he opened his mouth to dance around her statement again. "Don't you dare deny it. Who told you?"

Nathan gave a resigned sigh. "Cody came by this morning."

Disappointment stabbed through her. "And the deal with my father?"

Nathan's expression became a neutral mask. "It doesn't matter." He caught her arm when she spun away, stopping her flight. "You are pregnant with my child. And you will marry me."

Since Valentine's Day, she'd been beating herself up for letting him walk out of her life, wondering if by proposing with a diamond instead of a ring, he did realize how important her jewelry-designing was to her. That maybe he understood her at last.

Sure, he'd downplayed the emotional side of their arrangement, but considering how much he mistrusted love, she'd hoped that with time he'd come around. She'd gone to his office to tell him about the baby, eager to see if he'd missed her half as much as she'd missed him only to find out he had and that he still wanted to marry her.

Now, after learning that he'd only wanted to marry her because of the baby, she was heartbroken all over again.

"Nothing has changed, Nathan," she said. "I want a real marriage."

"Everything has changed. I'm not going to let my child grow up illegitimate." Nathan pulled her close. "And I'm not going to let another man raise my son or daughter."

The power of his conviction made Emma's knees wobble. Why couldn't he love her half as much as she loved him? It would make everything so simple. Even a hint of love would be enough for her to fling herself into marriage with him.

"I can't marry you knowing you don't love me."

"You can't raise this child on your own, Emma."

His lack of faith in her cut as deep as his inability to love her. She twisted free. "I'll be better off without you or my father telling me how I can't take care of myself. I'll continue to grow my jewelry business. Maybe I'll even open a shop."

"You don't need to work that hard." He set his hands on his hips and glowered down at her. "Marry me. I'll take care of you and the baby."

Emma stared at him for a long moment, her entire body aching to be held in his arms. It would be so easy to forget all her worries about money and raising a child on her own and accept his marriage proposal.

But she wasn't a practical person. And a marriage for practical reasons would break her heart.

She shook her head. "I'll take care of me. And the baby."

Twelve

We'll be just fine.

Emma's words reverberated through Nathan's head as he watched her disappear into the lunch-hour crowd. He didn't doubt for one second that she would be just fine as a single mother. She'd thrive the same way his mother had. They were both strong, capable women.

But what about him?

He wasn't going to be fine without her. Not one bit. For the first time in twenty years he needed someone more than he needed to breathe. Emma had become the center of his universe. For the last two weeks, he'd dwelled in a black hole of misery, deprived of her ready smiles, her sizzling looks and even her frowns. Instead of cradling her naked, soft, sweetly scented body in his arms, he spent his nights wide awake and wondering how everything had gone so terribly wrong.

Nathan took off after Emma, but it was too late. She'd vanished. Retrieving his car, he headed to her loft. But when he arrived, she wasn't there. Nor was she answering her cell phone.

He slammed his hand against the steering wheel. Dammit. Why did the woman have to be so stubborn? He could give her a wonderful life. They would be happy if only she'd stop holding out for something he couldn't give her.

After a fruitless visit to Addison, he called Cody and left a message. Out of options, Nathan headed home rather than returning to work. Knowing she was pregnant. Knowing he'd screwed up with her again. There was no way he could concentrate until he'd made things right with her.

He paced his empty condo for hours, watching the sun set, then rise. At seven, he seized his cell phone to try Cody a second time when it came alive in his hand. He answered the call without checking the number.

"Emma?"

"Not even close," his best friend said, sounding giddy and half out of his mind. "I got your message. Sorry I didn't get back to you sooner, but I've been a little busy watching my son being born."

Cody's words hit Nathan like a baseball bat. A son.

Was Emma carrying a boy, too? His lungs constricted as he considered all the things he'd miss if he couldn't convince her to marry him. He wouldn't be around when she felt the baby's first kicks. He wouldn't be there to fetch her all sorts of edibles in the wee hours of the morning as cravings hit her. And what if she didn't let him participate at the birth?

"Congratulations," he garbled into the phone, reeling at the unexpected punch of reality.

Misery tied his midsection in knots. *I love you.* Her words drilled into his head. A wake-up call he couldn't ignore.

She loved him. And he'd done nothing to deserve it.

She loved him. And all he'd offered her was a marriage based on logic and reason.

She loved him. And he'd not once admitted that he felt the same way. And he did. He loved her. Very much.

What a fool he'd been not to realize it before this. She'd enthralled his body and captured his heart, and he'd been too caught up in business schemes and ancient family history to see what was really important.

"Have you heard from Emma?" Nathan asked.

"She drove up last night."

Then Nathan was heading for Dallas as well. "What hospital are you in?"

He jotted down the address and threw some things in an overnight bag.

Four hours later, he left the car in the hospital parking lot and took a deep breath before heading up to the maternity ward. Finding Jaime's room, Nathan hesitated on the threshold and surveyed the tableau before him.

Cody sat on the edge of the bed, his back to the door, his attention split between the tired but radiant woman propped up by pillows and the bundle of blue cloth in a rolling bassinet. The pastel walls vibrated with the couple's happiness and jealousy rocked Nathan hard.

Emma was not in the room, and he was about to see if he could go find her, when Jaime spotted him and nudged her husband. Grinning like a lunatic, Cody left his wife's side to greet Nathan with a crushing handshake.

"How are you coping with fatherhood?" Nathan flexed his hand and scanned his friend's appearance, noting the dark circles beneath his eyes, the spot of throw-up on his shoulder.

"I've got the diaper-changing thing mastered."

"He's sleep-deprived," Jaime said, tossing her husband a fond smile.

Cody might be exhausted, but he looked happier than

Nathan had ever seen him. Which said a lot. Cody embraced life with more enthusiasm than pragmatism.

"Nathan, I'd like you to meet Evan Michael Montgomery." Cody scooped his son out of the bassinet, handling him with the same confidence he'd once handled a football. "Here, why don't you hold him?" With a sly grin, Cody deposited the fragile bundle into Nathan's hands. "Get in a little practice."

Nathan's stomach dropped to his toes at Cody's reminder of his own impending fatherhood. He stared at the newborn, marveling over his tiny fingers and toes. Would his son or daughter be this perfect? With Emma for a mother, why not?

Cody wrapped his arm around his wife. The look Jaime bestowed on her husband was equal parts pride, contentment and desire. Love. Nathan recognized the expression. But more than love. Completeness. As if together, the two were stronger than either could be on their own.

Would Emma ever look at him that way? Or had he blown his shot at deserving her love a dozen times or more already? Caught up in protecting himself from hurt, he hadn't wanted to admit that he needed her. He'd never let himself trust her the way Cody trusted Jaime.

From the beginning, he'd been the one to reject love and rely on more practical reasons to get married. But what Cody shared with Jaime wasn't just passionate love or friendship. It was deeper, more elemental. Permanent and unshakable.

"You're a natural," Jaime said. "You'll make a great father."

Yes, he would. And he'd make a great husband as well.

"So, what do you think of my son?" Cody asked, smiling down at the sleeping infant.

Nathan had a lump in his throat as he observed his happy friend. "I think you're the luckiest man alive."

* * *

Emma stopped the car in front of her father's house and braced herself for battle. The four-hour drive from Houston to the hospital in Dallas had given her plenty of time to sort through her jumbled emotions. She knew what to do about Nathan.

But first, she wanted to settle things with her father. She'd left the hospital after the briefest of congratulations because she wanted this confrontation behind her.

As she crossed the driveway to the front door, another car drove up. Nathan. What was he doing here? She waited for him at the foot of the steps, her heart bucking wildly as he advanced toward her.

"I don't want to fight with you," he said, drawing close enough to touch her.

She took a half step back, afraid if he took her in his arms, she would dissolve. "I don't want to fight with you, either." Side by side they climbed to the front door. "What are you doing here?"

Nathan opened the door so she could enter. "I know your father didn't give you back your trust fund."

"Cody." She shook her head as they crossed the grand hall, their footsteps echoing in the cavernous space. "Just once I wish my family would let me take care of things my way."

"Like telling me about the baby as soon as you knew you were pregnant?"

Grinding her teeth had become an all-too-frequent habit since Nathan had come back into her life. "Okay, I should have come to you sooner."

"You're damn right."

She cocked her head and regarded his stern expression and the uncompromising glint in his gray eyes. "But I had things I needed to think over."

"Such as reconsidering your refusal to marry me?"

"Can we have this discussion after I've gotten my father to agree to give me back my trust fund?"

"Let me help you with that."

"I can take care of it myself." They neared the hallway outside her father's study. She whirled on Nathan and put her hand on his chest. "You stay here. This is between my father and me. I need to do it alone." She emphasized the last word and hoped Nathan would stay put.

He captured her fingers and brought them to his lips for a quick kiss. Releasing her, he leaned his back against the wall and crossed his arms. "I'll be right here if you need me."

Heart tripping unsteadily, Emma gave a satisfied nod and walked on. The speech she'd prepared for her father vanished from her mind as she neared his study. The door stood open so she stepped in.

"Hello, Daddy."

Her father looked up from the papers on his desk. "Hello, Emma." He came to her, took her hands, and kissed her cheek. "How are you?"

"I'm fine." The words slipped out automatically. "I was at the hospital visiting your first grandchild. He's beautiful."

"I'm heading over in a few minutes," her father said, surveying her with a slight frown. "Are you sure you're all right?"

"I'm fine."

"Cody told me about the baby."

She was going to kill her brother.

"I hope you're here to tell me you're going to marry Nathan."

"I came by today to talk to you about our wager. I won. I want my trust fund back."

Silas frowned. "I don't want my grandchild growing up illegitimate."

"That's for Nathan and me to decide, not you." She met

her father's gaze, letting him see her determination. "I had the money by the deadline."

"But it wasn't in your account. So you forfeit. Now, what have you and Nathan decided about getting married?"

"That it's none of your business."

"But it *is* my business. I'm your father and I say you need someone to take care of you and the baby."

Emma kept her voice level. "I don't. I am perfectly capable of taking care of myself but you're too stubborn to see that."

"You think so? And how do you think you're going to do that without money?"

"I have money."

"Bah. The hundred thousand I gave you? How long do you think that's going to last?"

Emma shook her head. Stubborn old man. "Quite a long time, I imagine, since I'm not planning to live off it."

"No? Then how do you plan to support yourself?"

Emma braced herself against a wave of frustration and pulled the newspaper article about the Baton Rouge show out of her purse. She slapped it on the desk in front of him.

"This is about my jewelry. The article calls me 'brilliant' and describes my work as some of the finest around. I've worked hard for this recognition, and you've never given me any credit." She ran out of breath. With her heart pounding fiercely, she inhaled and spoke with deliberate force. "I'm good."

"You can't seriously expect to live on what you make from it."

Resentment injected steel into her voice. "I can. And I'm going to." She clenched her hands into fists so he wouldn't see how hard she was shaking. "You can keep my money. I don't need it. I'm going to make a go of my jewelry business. I'm going to take care of myself and my baby."

"Our baby." Nathan spoke the words softly from the

doorway behind her, but there was no denying the determination in his tone. "The baby is as much mine as it is yours, and you are going to marry me and let me take care of both of you."

Emma turned from her father and confronted Nathan. Everything inside her cried out to stop fighting him and let him take care of her. He held her heart in his hands. And now, with his child inside her body, she'd gone way past the point of trying to forget him and move on.

"We'll talk about that later."

"Putting me off isn't going to change my mind. I'm not letting you go. We belong together." He caught her by the arms. "Marry me," he whispered urgently. "Not because of the baby or a business deal, but because I can't live without you."

Joy seared her, sharp and unexpected, stealing her breath. She blinked away tears. Those words might be as close to a declaration of love as she would ever get from Nathan.

And it was enough. Nathan couldn't live without her. And she couldn't live without him. She'd been a stubborn fool to believe otherwise.

She cradled Nathan's cheek in her palm. "That's definitely something I want to discuss with you later. But first I need to settle things with my father."

Turmoil swirled in his gray eyes at her request. He wasn't the sort of man who backed down when he set his mind to something. But she was equally determined.

"But let me help you with this," he murmured.

It was a precarious tightrope that stretched between accepting help and standing on her own two feet. Could she trust herself and Nathan enough to achieve the right balance?

With her heart pounding dangerously fast, she wavered. She'd been fighting to stand on her own for so long that it was hard to stop. But for all her assertion that she could take care of herself, she liked having him to rely on.

Emma put her hand against Nathan's cheek as her sleepless night took its toll. Let him take care of you, her mind whispered. And at last she was ready.

"You can help," she said. "But just this once."

Teeth flashing in a mischievous grin, Nathan turned to her father. "She had the money on the fourteenth. I can attest to that. She refused to marry me because of it. And if you don't give her what she deserves for all her hard work, she will continue to refuse me out of a sheer stubborn need to prove that she doesn't need anyone to take care of her. Which, by the way, she's been doing really well for a long time, only none of us have given her credit for it."

Strengthened by Nathan's support, she confronted her father. "I want my money signed over to me as soon as possible. I have a nursery to decorate."

"And a wedding to plan," Nathan prompted, demonstrating that he wasn't kidding about persisting until she agreed to marry him.

"And if I don't?" Her father hadn't made his billions by being a poor negotiator.

"Then it will always be between us. I need you to look at me and see that I am a grown woman, capable of supporting herself. I deserve your respect because I earned it through hard work and determination."

Her father scowled, but Emma stood her ground until grudging approval transformed her father's expression.

"I only want the best for you," he said at last, his tone gruff, but gentle.

"I know you do." Emma gave him a weak smile. "And what's best for me is to know that you believe in me and in my ability to take care of myself."

"Very well. I'll give you your trust fund back. You did earn it, after all."

Emma mastered her shock before it showed on her face. Her knees weakened with relief. She pulled her spine straight.

"And no more interfering," she continued, capitalizing on her victory. "Meddling in my love life is wrong in so many ways." She pinned her father with a fierce scowl and waited until he nodded. Then, she turned to Nathan. "Daddy is going to visit his new grandson. I don't think he'll mind if we use his study while he's gone. You and I have a couple things to sort out."

Her father looked nonplussed at being ejected from his domain, but went without protest. As he passed Nathan, he paused and stuck out his hand. "Welcome to the family. I always liked you."

"Daddy!"

Once her father had exited the room and closed the door, Emma leaned against his desk and regarded Nathan.

"I'm sorry about the way I handled things earlier," he said. "I never should have let you walk away from me like that."

"I overreacted, too."

"You had cause. I've been acting like a stubborn fool."

"At last we agree on something." She took the sting out of her words with a smile and pushed off the desk. "Thank you for helping me out with my father."

He stood in place, his features like granite, but his eyes alive and wary as she advanced toward him one slow step at a time. "I'll always be there for you."

"I know that," she said, putting her hand on his chest and backing him toward the study door.

It no longer scared her that he might never love her the way she loved him. Nathan was the perfect man for her. He would honor their marriage vows and be a great father to their children. And when it came right down to it, she had enough love in her heart for both of them.

When his back met the door, Nathan stared into her eyes but made no attempt to touch her. "You should also know that the only merger that's going to happen between our families is you and me."

His announcement startled her. "After everything we've been through, you're not doing the deal with my father?"

"I don't want it to come between us," he said. "Plus, my brothers aren't ready for the sort of risk it involves and I've decided to stop fighting them on it."

"I don't understand." Her hand dropped away. "I thought you wanted to take over the company."

"I thought that's what I wanted, too. When my dad asked me to come back and help out Max and Sebastian, all I wanted to do was get back at them for the way they've always excluded me. But lately, I've realized that what I really want is to be accepted as part of the family."

Seeing the way his mouth curved downward, she leaned her body into his and framed his face with her hands. "How about becoming part of my family?"

At first, Nathan's expression reflected disbelief and hope. Then, his teeth flashed in a broad grin and his hands settled on her hips. "I think I've wanted that since the day you strutted past me in high heels and those ridiculous short shorts."

"I was sixteen." She regarded him in disbelief. "You turned me down flat, and I didn't see you again for ten years."

"I was way too old for you. I had to get out and stay gone. You scared the hell out of me." Lightning danced in his eyes. "You still do."

She was only half-ready for the arms that locked around her and pulled her up onto her toes. Her breath caught as his mouth claimed hers. Her body came immediately to life. She threaded her fingers through his hair and met the thrust of his tongue with matching passion while urgent encouragement issued from her throat.

She wanted him more than ever and wasn't afraid to let him know.

Nathan broke off the kiss and swept his lips toward her ear. "Sweet, sweet woman. I adore you."

His confession sparked a tremor inside her. She pushed

him to arm's length. "Say that again," she demanded, thinking she'd misheard him.

"I love you," he said, his smile softer than she'd ever seen it. "I'm sorry I didn't realize it sooner than I did."

She'd grown accustomed to his imposing will and powerful personality. But it was the tender expression on his face at that moment that made hope surge in her.

He loved her.

"But you said you didn't believe in love." The devilish quirk that weakened her knees returned.

"I believe in it. I just didn't want it in my life. With the exception of your brother and Jaime, everyone I've ever known has cheated on their spouse or been cheated on. After I moved in with my father's family, I watched my stepmother's love for him destroy her a little more each year. I was afraid to let that happen to me."

Emma recalled her own worries about how loving Nathan and keeping it to herself would eat at her. "What changed your mind?"

"You did. I couldn't understand how you could put such faith in love when you'd seen how miserable it made your parents. Then, yesterday, after finding out that you were pregnant, after you walked away, and today, seeing Cody and Jaime with Evan, I realized that having you in my life, in my bed, wasn't going to be enough unless I was in your heart and you were in mine. I love you."

"You do love me." Her voice trembled with awe.

"More than I ever thought it was possible."

He swept his lips across her eyes and down her nose. His hands slid over her curves, gentle, measuring caresses that awakened her to the quiet house and the lock on the study door. Desire rushed through her, sweeter than ever now that she knew Nathan loved her.

She eased her hands down the front of his shirt, loosening buttons as she went. Two weeks without him had been too long. She couldn't wait to get him naked and reacquaint herself with all those lovely rippling muscles.

"You know," she said, "I think my father is right after all. I do need someone to take care of me."

Nathan waited until she'd tugged the shirt down his arms and tossed it aside before he asked, "Got anyone in mind?"

"There was this really hot guy I met when I was a teen-ager." Enjoying the way her touch disturbed the cadence of his breath, she trailed her fingers down his chest and abdomen until she ran out of naked skin. "I wonder what ever happened to him."

When Emma started to unfasten his belt, Nathan caught her fingers and lifted them to his lips. "I think he finally figured out what's been missing in his life."

Soaking up the love and sincerity she saw in his eyes, Emma knew she'd found her happily-ever-after at last.

"And what's that?" she whispered.

Nathan's lips dipped toward hers. "You."

* * * * *

COMING NEXT MONTH

Available July 12, 2011

#2095 CAUGHT IN THE BILLIONAIRE'S EMBRACE
Elizabeth Bevarly

#2096 ONE NIGHT, TWO HEIRS
Maureen Child
Texas Cattleman's Club: The Showdown

#2097 THE TYCOON'S TEMPORARY BABY
Emily McKay
Billionaires and Babies

#2098 A LONE STAR LOVE AFFAIR
Sara Orwig
Stetsons & CEOs

#2099 ONE MONTH WITH THE MAGNATE
Michelle Celmer
Black Gold Billionaires

#2100 FALLING FOR THE PRINCESS
Sandra Hyatt

You can find more information on upcoming
Harlequin® titles, free excerpts and more at
www.HarlequinInsideRomance.com.

REQUEST YOUR FREE BOOKS!

2 FREE NOVELS PLUS 2 FREE GIFTS!

Harlequin Desire

ALWAYS POWERFUL, PASSIONATE AND PROVOCATIVE

YES! Please send me 2 FREE Harlequin Desire® novels and my 2 FREE gifts (gifts are worth about $10). After receiving them, if I don't wish to receive any more books, I can return the shipping statement marked "cancel." If I don't cancel, I will receive 6 brand-new novels every month and be billed just $4.05 per book in the U.S. or $4.74 per book in Canada. That's a saving of at least 15% off the cover price! It's quite a bargain! Shipping and handling is just 50¢ per book in the U.S. and 75¢ per book in Canada.* I understand that accepting the 2 free books and gifts places me under no obligation to buy anything. I can always return a shipment and cancel at any time. Even if I never buy another book, the two free books and gifts are mine to keep forever.

225/326 SDN FC65

Name   (PLEASE PRINT)

Address   Apt. #

City   State/Prov.   Zip/Postal Code

Signature (if under 18, a parent or guardian must sign)

Mail to the **Reader Service**:

IN U.S.A.: P.O. Box 1867, Buffalo, NY 14240-1867
IN CANADA: P.O. Box 609, Fort Erie, Ontario L2A 5X3

Not valid for current subscribers to Harlequin Desire books.

Want to try two free books from another line?
Call 1-800-873-8635 or visit www.ReaderService.com.

* Terms and prices subject to change without notice. Prices do not include applicable taxes. Sales tax applicable in N.Y. Canadian residents will be charged applicable taxes. Offer not valid in Quebec. This offer is limited to one order per household. All orders subject to credit approval. Credit or debit balances in a customer's account(s) may be offset by any other outstanding balance owed by or to the customer. Please allow 4 to 6 weeks for delivery. Offer available while quantities last.

Your Privacy—The Reader Service is committed to protecting your privacy. Our Privacy Policy is available online at www.ReaderService.com or upon request from the Reader Service.

We make a portion of our mailing list available to reputable third parties that offer products we believe may interest you. If you prefer that we not exchange your name with third parties, or if you wish to clarify or modify your communication preferences, please visit us at www.ReaderService.com/consumerschoice or write to us at Reader Service Preference Service, P.O. Box 9062, Buffalo, NY 14269. Include your complete name and address.

USA TODAY *bestselling author B.J. Daniels takes you on a trip to Whitehorse, Montana, and the Chisholm Cattle Company.*

RUSTLED

Available July 2011 from Harlequin Intrigue.

As the dust settled, Dawson got his first good look at the rustler. A pair of big Montana sky-blue eyes glared up at him from a face framed by blond curls.

A woman rustler?

"You have to let me go," she hollered as the roar of the stampeding cattle died off in the distance.

"So you can finish stealing my cattle? I don't think so." Dawson jerked the woman to her feet.

She reached for the gun strapped to her hip hidden under her long barn jacket.

He grabbed the weapon before she could, his eyes narrowing as he assessed her. "How many others are there?" he demanded, grabbing a fistful of her jacket. "I think you'd better start talking before I tear into you."

She tried to fight him off, but he was on to her tricks and pinned her to the ground. He was suddenly aware of the soft curves beneath the jean jacket she wore under her coat.

"You have to listen to me." She ground out the words from between her gritted teeth. "You have to let me go. If you don't they will come back for me and they will kill you. There are too many of them for you to fight off alone. You won't stand a chance and I don't want your blood on my hands."

"I'm touched by your concern for me. Especially after you just tried to pull a gun on me."

"I wasn't going to shoot you."

Dawson hauled her to her feet and walked her the rest of the way to his horse. Reaching into his saddlebag, he pulled out a length of rope.

"You can't tie me up."

He pulled her hands behind her back and began to tie her wrists together.

"If you let me go, I can keep them from coming back," she said. "You have my word." She let out an unladylike curse. "I'm just trying to save your sorry neck."

"And I'm just going after my cattle."

"Don't you mean your boss's cattle?"

"Those cattle are mine."

"*You're* a Chisholm?"

"Dawson Chisholm. And you are…?"

"Everyone calls me Jinx."

He chuckled. "I can see why."

Bronco busting, falling in love…it's all in a day's work.
Look for the rest of their story in

RUSTLED

Available July 2011 from Harlequin Intrigue
wherever books are sold.

HIEXP0711R